To Jack
& his Ma...

You will be
challenged
And find
Blessings.

Jim Fugate
3-21-08

EPIPHANY

James V. Ferguson M.D.

authorHOUSE®

AuthorHouse™
1663 Liberty Drive, Suite 200
Bloomington, IN 47403
www.authorhouse.com
Phone: 1-800-839-8640

First published by AuthorHouse 2/11/2008

ISBN: 978-1-4343-1492-5 (sc)

Printed in the United States of America
Bloomington, Indiana

This book is printed on acid-free paper.

This book is dedicated to my wife Becky, who always sees the best in me and has made me whole.

And a special thanks to my 1st editor, MLE

EPIPHANY:

a startling insight; a revelation or understanding that changes a
person's life; a moment of inspired clarity.

Anything you dream is fiction. Anything you accomplish is science.
The whole history of mankind is nothing but science fiction.

RAY BRADBURY

CHARACTERS

Humans/Terrans

Captain James Havel, 1st in command of exploration ship, *Odyssey*
Commander Steve Hinton, 2nd in command
Lieutenant John Woolsey, 3rd in command
Dr. Helen Tapp, Chief Medical Officer
Rebecca Havel, Director of Deep Space Exploration
Maj. Pat Marret, Professor Emeritus of the Space Academy
Dr. Emily Blair, Astrophysicist
Lu Farmer, Med-Surg nurse
MaryAnn Sams, Med-Tech Specialist
Ensign Dean Silber
Dr. Brown McCormick, Assistant Xenobiologist

Alpha Team:

Captain Havel
Dr. William Walker, Linguist
Dr. Linda Wade, Xenobiologist
Ensign Barbara Grubb, Navigation Officer and Pilot
Sgt. Raymond Parrott, Space Marines
Pvt. Stephanie Foulk, Space Marines
Pvt. Jeff Venable, Space Marines

Beta Team:

Commander Hinton
Ensign Joanna Wise, Chief Pilot
Dr. Jenny Snyder, Zoologist
Dr. Bert Nixon, Geologist
Sgt. Maj. Tom Cooper, Space Marines
Corp. Debbie Green, Space Marines
Pvt. David Grieves, Space Marines

Aliens

The People of the northern continent
Tenge—farmer, dreamer, husband
Kitu—Tenge's wife, mother of Roosa
Roosa—daughter of Tenge and Kitu
Rotan—head of the Village Council
Lamek—friend of Tenge, inventor
The Maker—divinity of the People

The Others of the southern continent
!Kirrt—panther-like hunter, female
!Zsakk—panther-like hunter, male
Ela—large herbivores preyed upon by Others

The Quixt—evolved race of beings throughout the galaxy
Quixt—member of the Quixt race and mentor of the aliens on G38-2
Progenitor—divinity of Quixt

PROLOGUE

In the beginning was the Word...
JOHN 1:1

The vast intelligence existed timelessly amidst an amorphous "foam" of possibilities. There was no past or future, only an infinity of present moments. The Mind floated within an existence of its own ideas and perceptions. At one point the Mind extended itself further, reaching with its senses, but reaching into what? The immense Consciousness suddenly realized that there was nothing but what it perceived. And then just as abruptly, the Mind came to the startling revelation that it was alone. A sense of yearning was conceived and then recognized as a desire for something beyond Itself.

New and expanding concepts began to form in the Mind. Emanations of thought began to push at the fabric of a proto-reality that would someday be the universe. The desire to extend Itself and to create suddenly resulted in the carving of energy from the primordial foam of its own existence. The Mind focused that energy, which then burst forth as a pulse of unimaginable intensity and power. The explosive wave of energy expanded rapidly from the Genesis Point creating both space and time as it spread outward—all at the direction and design of the Mind. As those expanding fires of creation cooled, they began to form the matter of the Cosmos. From a paradigm of thought a universe of reality and possibilities began—a universe of galaxies, worlds and creatures.

But there is more! The concept of *relationship* is also conceived by the Mind and then built into the fabric of the universe. That same unfathomable desire for relationship is at the core of all existence. Relationship is the nature of the Creator and its created.

CHAPTER 1

Miracles are not contrary to nature, but only contrary to what we
know of nature.
ST. AUGUSTINE

A torrent of neutrinos and charged particles flooded local space as the
giant starship exited the artificial wormhole eight hundred million
kilometers from the nearby yellow star. And just as suddenly as it
had formed the wormhole terminus collapsed, after belching an orb
of plasma-steel at a sub-relativistic velocity. If an observer had been
present at that place and time, he would have noticed nothing unusual
just seconds before the quantum engines of human ingenuity ripped
apart the fabric of local space-time. That same observer might have
perceived a subtle distortion in the background star pattern as the
forming wormhole began linking local space to a distant part of the
galaxy. Would he have been able to see down the wormhole's tunnel
as it stretched back across parsecs of interstellar space? Would he be
surprised to encounter such a phenomenon? Would he be forced
to dodge the hurtling space vessel as it raced forward at hundreds of
kilometers a second?

A sophisticated and philosophical observer of such an event
would undoubtedly wonder what kind of being is capable of controlling
such vast energies. What kind of creature is driven to journey across
space and time? An entity possessing such powerful knowledge and
technology would have to be investigated.

CHAPTER 2

Life is either a daring adventure, or nothing.
HELEN KELLER

"No matter how many times I do this it always gives me goose bumps," murmured Captain James Havel to himself. "To be in a place where no human has been—it never ceases to amaze me!" He made himself look away from the forward view screen and scan the instrument panels of the bridge. He watched his crew at their appointed jobs. But it was difficult to stay focused. He lapsed into reflection on everything that had brought his crew and him to this new place among the stars. He thought about the wonders of his age that allowed humans to travel across vast distances, virtually in an instant. "Truly amazing!" he thought as he shook his head slightly.

Havel reflected on the tingling sensations on the back of his neck that were now receding. His training told him that the quantum engines that created the artificial wormhole, which enabled his ship to traverse the alternative reality of sub-space and travel parsecs in an instant, were the cause of the physical sensation. "But then maybe some of the tingling is my own excitement," he smiled to himself. "We literally *jump* across light-years of normal space in an instant. How incredible is that?"

Havel remembered the first time he experienced the tingling sensations of excitement on the back of his neck. It was while traveling in Europe as a teenager. He guessed the sensation was from the excitement of going around the next bend and seeing something new

3

and perhaps wondrous. His high school traveling buddy quickly tired of "another Cathedral and another art museum." They had parted company physically and philosophically during that trip, as many high school friends do as they grow up. "Perhaps the sage is right," Havel thought. "'You can never go back.' And now here I am on the bridge of perhaps humanity's greatest technological achievement 'going around the next bend' to see what's out there. And the hair on the back of my neck still tingles every time we wind up the quantum engines and jump!"

Havel knew that making an artificial wormhole and accelerating a ship through its maw was one thing and quite another to do so and protect the ship and its crew from the roiling energies and the alternate reality of sub-space. Even the nature of that strange place within the wormhole was hotly debated in the officer's mess. One thing that was not debated was an appreciation of the technology that "allowed humans to go where they were never designed to be." Those same mighty engines that generated the wormhole also created a force field and a bubble of normal space-time that protected them while they were inside the wormhole. Havel smiled to himself, "Hell, this is both a dream and science. This is real science fiction!"

Havel could allow himself the luxury of reflection, knowing that his crew was the best. He watched them as they monitored the thousands of variables necessary to fly a starship. And from experience he knew that he was in fact maintaining an eye on things. He imagined it was somewhat similar to driving home safely at night and yet being detached from the details of the route. He always made it home safely even as his mind thought about the events of the day.

Havel admired the adventuresome spirit required of anyone who trusted this new Jump technology—its possibilities as well as its uncertainties. Havel and most of the crew had a working knowledge of the theories behind the wormhole, force fields, and the inter-dimensional reality of sub-space. But to sit in a machine and listen as the quantum coils wound up and formed the artificial wormhole was really "pretty gutsy," he thought. They literally jumped across light-years of space in an instant, "like taking a major short cut," he had explained to the media before the launch. "People, I'm really proud that my crew will ride with me on this adventure. It requires a Kirkegardian 'leap of faith' that we'll survive the transit through the alien environment of sub-space and then be able to reenter normal space, in one piece." He admitted to himself that it was a bit dramatic, but the media seemed to eat it up and it was good publicity for the Deep Space Program. Havel acknowledged that the physics, foundational for this wonderful technology, were beyond him and perhaps beyond all but a few truly gifted theoreticians. Smiling ruefully to himself, "and I'm not sure they really understand the whole process." But admittedly the technology seemed to work and humans for the first time were able to span the immense distances between star systems and worlds.

"And here I sit, doing something that others can only dream about," Havel thought. Yet he felt a connection to all those explorers before him who had gazed on foreign vistas. "I wonder if Coronado felt amazement when he first saw the Grand Canyon? And did Morton experience the same tingling sensation of excitement on his neck when his team landed beneath Mons Olympus of Mars? Do we fellow wanderers share more than our humanity when we *go where no one has gone before?*" he wondered as he thought back on the famous opening lines from the Star Trek series of the late twentieth century.

Havel always knew he had a wanderlust that his wife, Becky, could accept, but not really understand. She enjoyed going places with him, but not *the getting there*, as she referred to traveling. And now the two of them were physically further apart than either of them ever imagined. They had known from the start of their relationship that periods of separation would always be there. "Men have always gone to sea," Havel once quipped at their meeting twelve years ago at the Agency for Space Exploration (ASE). She told him later that she thought his remark was typical grandstanding of a "fly-boy". But their close professional collaboration in preparation for deep space missions had allowed her to see in him more than just bravado. The natural attraction was soon complemented by a mutual admiration and soon they were seeing each other regularly. He thought it was amazing that they had celebrated their tenth wedding anniversary just before *Odyssey* left on this second and longer voyage.

And fortunately for both of them the new "Jump" technology had changed everything relating to space exploration. They and everyone else at the ASE had expected a deep space mission to take years, if not decades. If Havel were selected for one of these missions they would be separated, perhaps indefinitely. But now a mission to local star systems would only take a few months!

Everyone saw this as a monumental advance, even Becky, since it was always her nature to see the positive in everything. But there was a downside as far as her career was concerned. The support systems for a deep space mission spanning years was very different than one for several months. Provisioning a starship would now be akin to providing for a nuclear submarine in the late twentieth century. Becky saw her field of nutrition and hydroponics, integral to long space voyages, rendered obsolete nearly overnight. "I'll go the way of the slide rule," she half-heartedly joked to Havel in their pillow talk.

But the ASE program leaders quickly found a way to use her many talents in other ways. Havel was really proud of her ability to adapt and this culminated in her appointment as the Program Director for the Deep Space Exploration branch of the ASE. How ironic that she would now direct the very exploration missions that he and other "fly-boys" would captain. Havel quipped that "she was now his boss," as if she hadn't been before.

A report from his executive officer, Steve Hinton, brought Havel out of his day dream. "Captain, the wormhole was successfully collapsed after our exit and the immediate sensor sweep reveals no electromagnetic transmissions or reaction drives. It looks like we're by ourselves, again."

"Thank you, Mr. Hinton."

Havel detected a sense of resignation in his executive officer's report. Though Havel knew from many late night discussions that they differed on the likelihood of finding sentient life, they frequently discussed and rehearsed first contact as part of their training. With another negative sensor sweep of another star system, Havel again wondered to himself if they would ever use their first contact training.

Many of the scientists aboard *Odyssey* were perfectly happy just doing basic research in the star systems they visited. But Havel believed that in the vastness of space surely humans would not be alone. At each new star system there was a chance, perhaps small, but a chance, that they might find other thoughtful beings. And Havel admittedly longed for this contact, even if this was not his ship's prime directive.

Everyone on the ship acknowledged that *Odyssey*'s primary exploration mission was to scout for habitable planets that might allow colonization and support some of the ever-increasing population of an overburdened Earth. Havel lamented that for all their technology, humanity in the mid 23rd century had not yet solved the insatiable desire of humans to procreate and consume. Therefore, space and worlds for expansion were sorely needed. In fact, many desired the challenges of the new frontiers of space to the crowded warrens of Earth. Even politicians considered expansion a better option than forced conservation and rigorous population control. These same politicians often found it easier to fund space exploration than to constantly tell their constituents *no*.

And the leaders of Earth were well aware of the limitations of conservation and equally aware of the finite resources in Earth's fragile and stressed ecosystem. Though fusion power technology had done much to solve the energy crisis and the environmental pollution of previous centuries, the ability to travel vast distances between stars created a new manifest destiny for humankind. The ASE was pleased when world leaders finally concluded that humans were destined to expand to the stars. It hadn't been so many years before that these same politicians were resistant to funding space exploration of the planets in the Sol system since significant colonization would always be so problematic. But now Jump technology opened up the possibilities of finding new pristine earth-like worlds for expansion.

Actually, Havel felt that humans were psychologically expansionist. In reading history he thought that humanity seemed to do better when expanding rather than in an introspective and static mode. A new era was dawning and humankind would no longer be confined to one planet, one island universe within a sea of stars and possibilities!

"Anything else, Steve?" Havel asked hopefully.

"No, Sir, nothing on the scans."

"Very well, continue to sweep the area and make sure that the Geophysics department has begun the initial survey of G38 and any planets in this system. Maintain passive scans only at this time."

"Aye, Captain."

7

"And Mr. Hinton, can't Dr. Blair in Stellar Cartography come up with a better designation for these star systems we visit? I mean the G designation for this star's energy output is clear. And this is the 38th star humans have visited, but it just seems so clinical and mundane."

"Well, Sir, this is the convention that the ASE came up with and the one we've been using. I guess we could change it, but then what should we use?"

"I'm not serious, Steve. I'm just carping a bit. I think I'll bug Dr. Blair to come up with something special if we ever find a star system and a world that is more than just a catalog notation."

Havel liked the affable Hinton, as did most of the crew. And he was also a good officer. Havel thought they made a good team, even though they were still getting used to each other, the ship, and the crew. There was certainly a learning curve to driving a starship and managing its complex mixture of Space Navy and scientist crew. No amount of in-system training and short jumps could replace the interdependency the crew now felt after two months of numerous jumps and being fifty light-years from Earth and home.

Odyssey was a prototype of the new class of starships humans designed to take humans to the star systems closest to Earth, especially those systems that had Sol-like stars. The teardrop design was ideally suited for the vacuum of space, since there was no need of aerodynamic requirements. Havel remembered the physicists droning on and on about the optimal configuration of a ship to generate and sustain a wormhole. Actually, he felt the elliptical design had a certain esthetic appearance, but more importantly the design meshed well with the requirements of the warp coils encircling the ship.

But generating a wormhole was one thing. Technology was also necessary to push the fifty thousand metric ton space ship through the hole in space-time and to protect the fragile cargo of humans in the alternative reality of the sub-space. In fact the need to shield humans from the alien environment drove the technological development of stasis field generators. These engines worked to provide a protective force field bubble around the ship and shield them all from being torn apart by the violent forces in the wormhole and the hard vacuum of sub-space. Personally, Havel was just glad that artificial gravity was a by product of the stasis field technology. He never liked the sensation of perpetually falling in the zero gravity of space. Many people like his wife, Becky, could never get accustomed to free-fall. With a degree of tongue-in cheek he thought, "I wonder what allows some people to adapt to the sensation of having their stomachs up in their throats all the time?"

The *Odyssey* and her sister ship, *Pegasus,* were primarily designed as exploration and research vessels. Their designs were similar and encompassed twenty decks of living quarters for the 100 crew members, science labs, engineering and navigation equipment, and the forward bridge pod. Additionally, the artificial gravity gave the crew a natural *up and down* orientation in the ship. Finally, the huge problem of osteoporosis, due to prolonged weightlessness, had now been largely overcome by the maintenance of Earth-like gravity.

But *Odyssey* was more than a survey and research vessel. Havel had been part of the design process and had insisted on some military capabilities. He argued, "We'll be a long way from home and we can't call for back up if we run into trouble." Some had argued that this was a waste of money because many still clung to the notion that humans were alone in the universe. But thankfully this was a minority position and so the ships were outfitted with the latest design of maser canon and upgrades to the energy screen generators making them highly capable of dissipating energy weapons. Kinetic weapons and nukes would still pose real problems, but an emergency jump was thought to be the best defense for the ship if *Odyssey* encountered these types of threats. *Odyssey* herself possessed a small number of missiles with nuclear warheads, but "God forbid if we ever need them," thought Havel.

Havel continued his reflection as he waited for additional reports to come into the bridge. "What a surrealistic way to travel. We create a wormhole torus of folded and warped space-time and then push our ship through this alternative dimension using the sub-relativistic inertia we carry into the hole; all the while protecting our butts by maintaining an oasis of normal amid the roiling energies of subspace!"

"That's not bad prose," he thought to himself. "Maybe I should jot down some of my thoughts in a journal and write a book someday. Yeah, sure!" he smiled to himself. "It might make a good story to think about how we trust science or the calculations necessary to judge where we'll be when we exit the wormhole. I wonder what would happen if we can't turn the damn field off and collapse the wormhole when we exit the terminus and return to normal space."

"Long distance stellar and geological surveys are under way, Captain," said Hinton. "All decks are reporting nominal conditions after the last jump. Dr. Blair in Stellar cartography estimates that the last jump was seven parsecs. That beats our previous record, Captain."

"Very well, Mr. Hinton; make sure engineering is recharging the warp generators. I want the fusion reactors to remain at ninety percent output in case we have to jump clear. I take it there was no apparent strain on the ship or crew despite the sizeable jump?"

"No reports of problems, Captain. Maybe the only limit to our jump capability is our ability to predict where we'll emerge from the wormhole. The theorists tell us we're safe to move inter-dimensionally over any distance and even through a star! But that seems pretty dicey to me. The real issue is positioning the wormhole terminus. What if the wormhole's end is in a small planetoid or near a star's gravity well?"

"Where's your trust, Steve?" kidded Havel, feigning surprise. "The physicists say that the problem is forming the warp field near a massive object or in positioning the terminus too close to a sizable mass. They say that if the terminus is too near a massive body the wormhole either won't form or it'll be so unsteady that we'd be able to detect the problem and make adjustments before we enter the proximal end."

"Well, I know that's what they say, Sir, but…"

Havel held up his hand, "I'm just kidding, Steve! The experts aren't flying this ship *through* stars or planets. Sub-space may be multi-dimensional and not exist in the same realm as normal space, but it's just a bit too much to tell us to not worry about flying through a star or returning to normal space inside of one! We've had this theoretical discussion before and I'm with you. I want to be damn careful as we learn all the nuances of this technology and our capabilities," said Havel. "The theorists are fifty light-years away and aren't riding this horse. So we'll just make certain there's nothing along our flight path before we jump."

Havel purposely spoke a little louder than was necessary and glanced around the bridge as he spoke so that not only his Exec could hear him, but other bridge crew could as well. "We need to take great pains in our plans before we jump because, as you know, Steve, all our pre-jump projections are based on observations that are years old. Just think about it. You just reported that our final jump into this system was seven parsecs or twenty one light-years. Our calculations for the terminal jump into this system were based on the position of G38 before our last jump. Light had to travel for twenty one years across normal space to our last point of observation. So we make projections on where we'll exit the wormhole based on data that is twenty one years old! Mind boggling isn't it? And then we jump across that gulf in a fraction of ship time! It never ceases to amaze me that we are no longer bound by the speed of light, even though our measurements are! What do you think Albert Einstein would say about that, Steve?"

"He might have to pick up his false teeth from the floor, Captain," smiled Hinton. "It is really amazing …and wondrous," said Hinton with uncharacteristic wistfulness as he looked toward the view screen, his voice trailing away.

Again, speaking to everyone within ear shot, "Yes, it surely is." Looking around at his staff Havel seized on a teachable moment. "Many of you may think we have too many regulations, but I believe several are critical. We make several deep space jumps traveling to a new star, but the last jump into a planetary system is the toughest. Interstellar space is very empty, but planetary systems are full of objects. We have no way of determining whether small but potentially dangerous mass might be in our flight path as we exit the wormhole. And what if we jumped into a system inhabited by a belligerent and intelligent alien? So I'm glad we have regulations, and I'm glad that *Odyssey* will be able to defend herself if we find someone else out here."

His Exec rose to the bait and said, "Now Captain, we've been over this a dozen times. There's just no evidence of sentient life even after centuries of study. Look at the SETI (Search for Extraterrestrial Intelligence) project; it was a big zero. And we've found nothing noteworthy in more than three dozen planets we've studied, some at close range. I'll believe we're not alone when I see some data," Hinton finished with an air of certainty.

Listening to the conversation, Lt. John Woolsey couldn't resist the opportunity to speculate with his superior officers. "Commander Hinton, there must be advanced life somewhere. The universe is just too big to think we're alone. The problem is that the distance between the stars is so huge that, until jump technology, we were just so isolated."

"A good point, Mr. Woolsey," said Havel. "Now we'll have the chance to test that hypothetical speculation. We'll be able to bridge those vast distances that isolate worlds and perhaps civilizations. As you all know this has always been an interest of mine."

Thinking back, Havel recalled late night college debates, over pizza and beer, on the issue of causality. That philosophical, questioning attitude was still with him, though he found that late night pizza and beer was not a good thing to do after age thirty.

"Mr. Woolsey, do you recall the Augustinian concept of causality?"

"Yes Sir, I think it relates to a perspective that we're here because of our parents, going all the way back to our origins."

"Very well said, John. The question is where is the beginning? Is there a genesis point? Is there a reason for our existence or is all we see just chance?"

Havel continued, "I once speculated in an Academy paper that the reason stars are so far apart was to keep sapient life away from each other until a species was advanced enough for contact with other thoughtful creatures. Perhaps our science and technology will afford us a new perspective on the universe, one that has spiritual connotations. This leads to another consideration, Mr. Hinton. If we ever find thoughtful life, what do you think that will do to the fragile human psyche or our religious institutions?"

"Now Sir, you know that I respect your opinions, but you also know that I find the spiritual perspective totally illogical. I do believe that if we ever encounter sapient aliens we'll be ready. As for religion, it'll be a shock to those with the most rigid ideologies, but I don't believe contact will affect most of us," said Hinton confidently.

"Yes, I know where you stand, Steve. The question was more of a rhetorical one for Mr. Woolsey."

Thankful for being included in the discussion, Lieutenant Woolsey said emphatically, "Captain, we'll eventually find thoughtful beings. And I believe it will definitely have an effect on us as a species and on our institutions. This will be a momentous event for humanity and for those of us who see a spiritual aspect of reality."

"I think you're right, John. We can't predict how this will affect us, but I'm convinced it will," said Havel.

He and Becky had often discussed whether humans were special, and whether they were "created in God's image" as some said. If another civilization were discovered, that was even more advanced than humans or had their own solipsistic perspectives, what would that do to humanity's notion of preeminence? Havel felt that he and his crew were as trained as possible for first-contact, but "can anyone really be ready?" he wondered to himself.

Hinton was correct; missions so far had found life, though nothing more advanced than lichenoids and other simple plant-like species. During this voyage *Odyssey* had already visited nine other star systems with G and K type suns, and energy outputs similar to Sol. They had performed their obligatory cataloging of these systems, and even found a few planets that might be worth closer study later or possible terra forming as a step toward eventual colonization. But there had been no signs of any life that really excited anyone except perhaps the scientists. But Havel just *knew* there must be advanced life in the Cosmos. He had asked the question a million times, "Why should there be thoughtful creatures on only one planet, circling one star, in the backwaters of one galaxy, among the hundreds of billions of known galaxies?" The problem was well articulated by his third in command; the vast distances between stars and other planetary systems left Earth isolated like an island in the midst of a vast sea. Havel kept telling himself that he must be patient. After all this was only the second mission for *Odyssey* and together with her sister ship, *Pegasus*, just thirty seven star systems had been visited in the last two years. He knew in his gut that there must be other sentient life somewhere in the vastness of the universe. "Why would God create thoughtful life in only one place and one time?" he rationalized over and over again in his mind. "There are four hundred and fifty billion stars in the Milky Way alone and we know there are more than 100 billion galaxies in the

Cosmos. There must be thoughtful life somewhere," he concluded for the thousandth time.

Hinton broke into Havel's reflection with a systems report. "Sir, the jump generators are recharged and engineering reports the reactors are nominal. I'm getting the preliminary specs from our long distance surveys. There appear to be seven planets in this system."

Havel noted the extra hint of excitement in his executive officer's usually cool voice. It was Hinton's job to scan the data from the various departments reporting to the bridge. His professional voice returned as he read out the data streaming to his bridge station. "Five of the outer planets are gas giants. There's an inner planet that has a dense core and a magnetic moment suggestive of iron, but is too close to the sun to be realistically habitable and doesn't seem to have an atmosphere."

Havel noted that Hinton's voice seemed to rise a fraction of an octave as he continued to report on the data. "There is one planet approximately one hundred and fifty million kilometers from G38. It appears to be 1.1 Earth's diameter and seems to have an atmosphere and a magnetic core! It looks promising, Captain, especially because it's in the habitable range from the sun. I'd recommend we make a closer survey."

"Well that's what we're here for, Commander, but it'll take us three days and considerable reaction mass to orbit the planet. Then we'll have to climb back out of the inner system gravity well to be clear enough for another jump. Is this still your recommendation?"

Havel was not baiting his executive officer as much as he was encouraging him to make a commitment to a course of action. Decision making was integral to leadership and an officer's development. Havel personally hated all fly-bys, probably more than any of the crew. He always wanted a closer look at the non-gas planets they encountered. However, energy and time constraints required considerable prudence and conservation of reserves. Though the ship was outfitted to support its human cargo for up to six months, the number of systems they visited in each voyage depended on whether they made their surveys from a distance or whether closer inspection was required of a promising planet. Dual fusion reactors supplied *Odyssey's* principal energy needs, including the jump generators and the ship's weaponry. But *Odyssey's* primary in-system propulsion was an ion drive. This system moved *Odyssey* by accelerating charged particles through the tail exhaust vent. Since the drive mass for the ion engine was hydrogen brought from Sol's own gas planets, and was ordinarily non-replenishable, they had to be selective in their orbital insertions. Theoretically they could harvest hydrogen from any gas planet, but it was not something that had been done by a starship. Harvesting hydrogen was usually done by atmosphere-capable space craft that dipped into the upper atmosphere and scooped up hydrogen.

As Havel waited for his Exec to make his final recommendation, he considered the tactical problem of an orbital insertion. Because massive objects like suns and planets distorted the fabric of space and time, regulations proscribed the safe use of the jump engines one hundred and fifty million kilometers from any star. So an orbital insertion would bring them close to G38 and might cut off his escape in the event of trouble. Theoretically, they could still try to form a wormhole and jump while in-system, but it was thought to be dangerous. Havel hoped he would never be forced to test those safety parameters and try to form a wormhole that close to a planet or a star. He also realized that jump coordinates could be distorted by the gravity well of a planet or sun. It might be anyone's guess where a ship might end up after such a desperate maneuver.

"Sir, I believe this planet has real potential, and it's within the mission specs for a closer observation." This time Hinton spoke in a less excited and more poised voice. "Captain, I'm also measuring some additional energy patterns from the planet, but I can't make any conclusion with only passive scans," he reported without looking up from his instrument panel.

"I agree with your recommendation, Mr. Hinton; let's get a closer look at G38-2; I believe that would be Emily Blair's taxonomy. I'll also authorize active scanning to study the second planet as we spin down.

"Aye Captain," came Hinton's somewhat relieved response.

"Ensign Wise, plot an orbital insertion vector for us. When you've got the navigational computer programmed, notify engineering to light up the ion drive and take the jump engines off line as we begin our approach," Havel ordered.

"Aye, Sir; Course plotted!"

Turning again to his Exec, Havel said, "And Steve, charge our weapon systems as standard protocol mandates with an orbital insertion. Mr. Woolsey, please notify the crew and all science labs that we are spinning down to take a closer look at the second planet. Let's make the most of our visit to this corner of the universe, folks!"

CHAPTER 3

There are more things in Heaven and Earth than are dreamt of in
your philosophy.
SHAKESPEARE

Quixt was suddenly aware of a massive space-time distortion
approximately seven hundred and fifty million kilometers from his
position. "What the hell is that?" he thought to himself, as he extended
his sensory array to study the anomaly. As he analyzed the gravitational
distortion, he concluded that the anomaly must be due to a wormhole.
And then just as suddenly the gravity waves were gone, but he still
detected a massive object in that region of space that he was sure had
not been there before. He thought to himself, "These unusual readings
have got to be related." And just as quickly he surmised that the best
explanation for the events was the presence of a space vehicle exiting an
artificial wormhole. The ability to form a wormhole and travel inter-
dimensionally could only mean a traveler with a very high order of
technology and sentience. This had never happened to Quixt before.
He scanned his extensive data banks and he could find no description
of a space traveler ever entering a system where one of his kind was
working.

Quixt had been in this star system for several hundred cycles
observing the second planet and aiding the development of its
inhabitants. His initial reaction to the intruder was one of surprise
and then intense curiosity. He had to investigate a life form that could
create and control such power! But as he made plans to investigate the

anomaly, he admitted to himself that he was also apprehensive—not for himself, but for the beings on the second planet below him whose destinies might forever be changed by the arrival of a starship.

Quixt's ancestors had once been corporeal, star-faring beings. But the Progenitor had transformed his ancestors eons ago, over thousands of millennia, into beings without a bodily form and then set them to work among the stars. They called themselves collectively the *Quixt,* though the derivation of that term was now lost in the mists of time. The *Quixt* now existed as an energy matrix, without a home and without a body to impede them in their travel between the stars or hinder their work. Their unique function was to find promising life forms and aid the development of these life forms toward full sentience. The *Quixt* were like farmers who nurtured and cultivated their crops. The universe was full of life, but only a small percentage of life forms were capable of full sentience. The *Quixt* focused their efforts on those species with the highest capacity for development. It was these special few that the *Quixt* helped to raise to a level of self-awareness and curiosity that one day they might ask the crucial questions, "Why am I here? What is my purpose?" These questions were foundational to a relationship with the Progenitor. Eons ago the *Quixt* species accepted the challenge from the Progenitor and adapted to what they ultimately considered to be their noble and sublime destiny. Quixt had often reflected on his origins and his appointed task. He always ended with the rational conclusion, "How could you argue your fate when it was orchestrated by God?"

Though he worked alone, Quixt was *aware* of others of his species in distant parts of the galaxy. But he had no direct communication with these other *Quixt* entities. They operated in star systems that were vast distances from the yellow sun where he now worked. Quixt's perceptions of his kind were mostly sensed as their collective struggle against entropy. This passion to struggle against ever lower energy states was fundamental to the *Quixt.* Quixt often imagined life as anti-entropic. Organized life was actually a violation in a principle of physics where all energy systems moved to lower energy states. He thought, "If all physical systems tend to a lower energy state, why does life evolve to a higher order?" His only conclusion was that "there had to be something that promoted life to this higher level. Perhaps it is we *Quixt* who are responsible. But then who helped us advance?" And so the mind games of logic and causality went round and round in his mind during moments of reflection. But he always came back to the only plausible answer that something had to be first. *Perhaps it was you, my Lord,* he prayed into the black void around him.

Though travel between the stars was not especially difficult for Quixt and his species, it was energy draining; and the *Quixt* abhorred wasting energy that did not directly serve their prime directive and function. The stars were so distant and therefore the *Quixt* were solitary creatures. He did not think of himself as being lonely, in the sense that corporeal creatures might understand. In fact the creatures whom he assisted gave him company enough, he thought. His work was his life. It gave him direction and purpose, and he felt at peace with the Progenitor, his Creator and his God.

Quixt understood that his prime directive was the advancement of life. He was driven by the belief that the Progenitor desired that all life should come to know the Creator and be in relationship with Him. A caring and loving Creator that desired connection and relationship with those created was the philosophy that had motivated the transformation of the *Quixt* and sent his kind to tend the fertile fields of the stars.

Quixt often thought of himself as a shepherd, a term that he coined long ago on another world. His work then was with a group of beings he called Terrans. Those beings nurtured and herded a quadruped animal they called sheep. As he nurtured the minds of those herders of sheep, it occurred to him that he was somewhat of a shepherd himself, only on a much grander scale. He thought, "Those Terran shepherds still remain special in my memory." He remembered how they had flourished under his tutelage and rose rapidly along the developmental scale to ever higher levels of thoughtfulness. Quixt admitted to himself that his results with those Terrans had become the benchmark for his work everywhere.

There had been other promising proto-sentient species on that ancient planet that were developing alongside the Terrans. He worked with those creatures as well, but eventually Quixt felt compelled to move on to the next star system when it became obvious that the sheep herders would be the dominant species. Quixt recalled his departing

19

thoughts so long ago. "Someday the sheep herders will look up at the stars and wonder about their place in the order of things. They will eventually ask the critical question, 'Why am I here?'" He hoped that the spark sewn in the other species known as apes and dolphins would someday flourish and that they too would come to wonder "Why?"

It had been a long time since Quixt had thought about those ancient inhabitants of Terra. He wondered what had triggered this ancient memory. It was true that once he had felt very close to all those creatures, perhaps more so than others he had nurtured. But the time had come to let go and move on and he did so without remorse. Quixt recalled the Terran story of one called *Johnny Appleseed*. Quixt thought of himself as a proverbial *Johnny Appleseed* of the Galaxy. Sow and move on; that was the way of the things.

His current work was with the inhabitants of the second planet in this star system—a water world with two very isolated continents. This afforded Quixt an unusual challenge and opportunity. The separation of these two landmasses had allowed the evolutionary development of several proto-sentient species on different continents in virtual isolation.

The *People* on the northern continent were especially promising. They possessed inherent empathetic traits that had blossomed into full telepathic abilities with Quixt's help. However, Quixt found it troubling that they now seemed to be developmentally stuck with little curiosity beyond their appreciation of each other and their bucolic Eden-like existence. It was a delicate balance to gently stir their hearts and alter their minds without causing damage. Subtly enhancing dendritic connections in a being's brain was a delicate process, Quixt knew. He had been too impatient on other worlds with disastrous results of insanity and death. And now the telepathic ability of the *People* made his work even more tedious because any change in one being often affected another in unpredictable ways. "Maybe I've erred again," he worried. "And maybe my zeal has caused their complacency."

But to his relief there was some progress lately. Several of the *People* were acting on their ideas and one young male named Tenge was especially imaginative. Quixt hoped that in another generation or so the balance would shift and the *People* would move forward to an even higher order of thoughtfulness. "Perhaps some day I'll be confident that the *People* will advance sufficiently to seek the Progenitor on more than their current shamanistic level," Quixt thought.

His work on the other continent was lagging behind that of the *People*. As a result he was beginning to focus more and more of his attention on Tenge and the *People* and less on those who called themselves the *Others*. But progress had occurred even with these aggressive hunters, so he reminded himself that he must be patient and not allow his passion to overcome his basic logical and methodical nature. Time, he reminded himself again and again, was not as important as the eventual outcome.

The advanced energy matrix of Quixt's mind processed his reflections almost instantaneously. And now the arrival of what must be a star-faring entity into the system where he was working potentially changed everything. There were many advanced life forms in this spiral arm of the Galaxy, but he had never been present in a system where there was the potential of contact between a technologically developed species and one of dawning sentience. Surely this must have occurred in other places over the 14 billion years of the Progenitor's creative and emotive force, but there was no record of this in his experience or in the *Quixt* data banks.

Is this mere chance or part of your Great Design? he prayed into the blackness of space as he analyzed the situation and his options. *Tell me, Lord, what I should do. Should I prevent the inevitable contact between the interlopers and the creatures of this world? Should I prevent the inevitable contamination? Perhaps I should try and orchestrate the encounter to minimize the external influence? But am I not an external influence on these beings? Could this be a test of my faith and trust in the Great Plan?*

"Ah, Quixt, questions and prayers cast into the silent darkness again," he sighed. With a bit of frustration fueled by his indecision Quixt said, *I wish you would just answer me sometime and reassure me.* Quixt, time and again, indulged himself with a dialogue with the ever silent Progenitor. Quixt admitted to himself that he occasionally sulked because, though he often asked for some sign, he had never received any overt response from the darkness of space around him. Sometimes in his musings though, he came upon what he sensed was a direction.

It was at these moments of clarity or epiphany that he felt most sure of the Way and the Progenitor's Great Design.

"Enough philosophy, Quixt; it's time to act." Quixt focused his mind and energies and shifted inter-dimensionally to a position approximately five thousand kilometers from the latest addition to the solar system. He scanned the interloper and confirmed his speculation that the object was indeed a space vessel. He kept himself hidden by remaining in a higher dimensional state than normal reality. As he probed the Artificial Intelligence in the ship's computer he was reassured that these creatures were explorers and had a high regard for all life. The beings were corporeal, bipedal, but there was something else about them that he just couldn't quite resolve; it was like a perception or a thought just on the edge of being remembered or clear.

His immediate concern was whether these creatures would respect the inhabitants of the planet. It was a gamble to let things progress, but he sensed a certain rightness of the situation. He really couldn't explain why he felt this way; "it is really quite illogical," he told himself. He could certainly stop the ship before it got to the second planet, but should he? His mind worked furiously over the problem and suddenly he sensed his answer, perhaps from the void. "I must trust my instincts on this and allow the inevitable contact. I must trust in the Design; I must reach out in faith!"

CHAPTER 4

If we always look down we will never see the stars.
HAKUIN

Alpha Continent

The Sun felt warm on Tenge's back as he turned the fallow ground of his field outside the Village. It was good to be out in the fields again after the *Cycles of Water*. The periods of rain and the forced inactivity made him restless and appreciate the end of the rainy season. "Everything is so lush again," he sighed in quiet appreciation of his world, especially noting the deepened colors of the well watered forest.

His spade sank again easily into the ground that still had some looseness from the previous season's cultivation. He noted that the soil was moist even a half ferl underneath the surface. "I'll bet the wetness will make it hard to use Lamek's new gadget," he thought to himself. He had borrowed the device from his neighbor after hearing of Lamek's success tilling his field last fall. Tenge thought again how odd it was for Lamek to come up with such a novel idea. Lamek told him that the idea just came to him at the end of the last growing season. Tenge thought, "Lamek's a great guy, but he's not a thinker and certainly not one to tinker something together." And the name he chose for his contraption was equally strange; he called the thing a *plow*. Tenge had asked him why he chose this word and Lamek said it just seemed the right name for the contraption.

It occurred to Tenge that a lot of the People seemed to be making discoveries lately. The elders just passed off the new perspectives as a result of their leadership, but Tenge didn't think so. He considered the elders just a bunch of "politicians," as a hiss escaped involuntarily from his lips. His wife, Kitu, was convinced that the innovations in the Village were due to the Maker's kindness and favor. But this was always Kitu's somewhat simplistic answer to most things. He let it go and sought the solitude of his labors where he had time to think and sort things out. He often thought about things as he lifted and turned the dark soil of his field. "Maybe I'll figure it all out some morning here in the field," he smiled to himself as he dug deeply and turned the rich soil.

He enjoyed solitude perhaps more than most. It gave him time to extend his mind and sense the trees, the animals in the forest, and, even more distantly, others of his Village as they also worked their fields. He could tell what his fellow Villagers were thinking and feeling, especially if he took pains to focus his mind in a specific direction. But it was considered impolite to probe the thoughts of others if there was no need for dialogue, so he quickly redirected his mind. He often wondered why the Maker favored the People and blessed them with a complexity of thought that was so different from the creatures in the forest. Kitu and the shamans said that his People were different because they were the "chosen ones" as described in the sacred texts. He wasn't sure that this was the entire answer, but he couldn't argue with the observation that those of his kind were more thoughtful and successful than any other creature of the World. Whatever the reason, he was glad to be able to sense the life force in all living things and the connection that everything had to the whole. He told Kitu that his appreciation of the World was a manifestation of the Maker. This simple proclamation of his faith had made her smile. He knew she loved him and tolerated his philosophical musings. Hers was truly a "simple faith," and he had to admit that her approach to life seemed to cause less anxiety and more happiness than his struggles to understand. Tenge often wondered if it was better to just accept things as Kitu and his neighbors seemed to do with ease.

Tenge reached out with his mind and felt the *balance* in the World around him. He felt as though he were a part of everything else and he again acknowledged the great satisfaction this gave him. "It's peaceful here in the field, almost spiritual," he thought to himself.

He knew from the old stories that the People had felt this connection to the World for such a long time that Tenge feared it was now taken for granted. Tenge felt that the People's ability to *understand without speaking* gave them a unique ability to connect to each other as well as the whole. Somehow he sensed this was special and should never be taken for granted. He knew from the ancient stories that his People once used their mouths to communicate. Now, it was only the children who laughed and yelled noisily with their mouths until they passed into adulthood at the Awakening Ritual and connected with the Village. He remembered his own passage, when his mind was opened to the collective thoughts of the Village, its heritage and the common knowledge. Tenge had thought about the ritual many times and still did not understand how children were suddenly able to share feelings and thoughts with the adults of the Village. The shamans and elders said this wonder was from the Maker. "But how did the People first learn to understand and speak with their minds?" he asked. But no one else seemed to know how this occurred or care why.

And yet for all their closeness, Tenge sensed that the People needed something more. Maybe it was drive or maybe it was just a curiosity that he alone seemed to possess. He often looked up at the *lights of the night sky* and wondered about his World. It was then that dreams and thoughts of other places, other times, and even other thinking creatures more complex than those of the forest, would come to him. He had tried talking to Kitu about his musings, but she didn't understand his thoughts. She told him on more than one occasion that she had no need of such thoughts.

"The Village is here and now and that is all that is important," she said. "The only *other place* is across the Great Waters, and that is such an old tale that it must be a myth. No one could have journeyed to such a distant place, especially across the sea."

The village elders were especially critical of his musings and questions. "What is the point of your dreams? How will this help the next crop or our Village?" they asked. The elders taught the ancient scriptures and what was "important," they said. And the shamans said that the Maker had given the scriptures and understanding to the People long ago on the Holy Mountain. But after studying the scriptures Tenge felt that he just needed more explanation than the scriptures and elders could provide him. He often wished that he had the faith of Kitu, and then he would be able to see through the inconsistencies of the ancient stories and not be so tormented by doubts. "I'd be happier," huffing as he dug, "if I were just like everyone else and didn't have questions."

The sacred legends and the Holy Scriptures held that the People were on a "great boat" floating forever on the Great Waters, a sea that was so vast that no one who sailed over the horizon ever retuned. Tenge wondered if there were other places over the horizon, but the common wisdom held that there was no way to know and therefore it was useless to speculate on a subject that had no answer. "But it matters to me!" he would say. The questions were a part of his being. The fact that others didn't care or weren't even curious was disturbing to him.

As Tenge worked, his mind wandered outward from the simple repetitive task of digging, to touch the minds of the animals in the forest around him. The People called the third eye, at the apex of their triangular heads, their *Seeing Eye*. Tenge literally "looked" into the minds of the forest animals and registered their simple thoughts as emotions of fear, hunger and mating instincts. Though their thoughts were simple, they collectively afforded him a panoramic view of his immediate area. With a little practice he had mastered the ability to organize their multiple and disparate perspectives and triangulate his own position through their collective eyes.

He often enjoyed seeing himself through the eyes of the animals. "There I am," he thought to himself. He saw himself working in the field using his arms to dig with his spade. He observed his brindle colored fur that he knew was no longer necessary as camouflage. The People were the dominant species in the World and weren't threatened by any other animal. The animals of course did not understand what he did in the field or why he wore the tanned coverings over his body. Their primitive minds were not sophisticated enough to consider such things. They watched him curiously and cautiously from the treetops and the edge of the nearby forest. Tenge considered their perspective of his powerful running legs. He didn't see his legs to be as long as the animals perceived them. Tenge contemplated his manipulating hands holding the spade. "Those hands had once held weapons," he thought to himself, but that was long ago. There was no need for warfare any longer. There was more than enough for everyone. "Perhaps we are the Maker's chosen ones."

As he continued to observe himself he recalled his latest question to the Elders. "Why are the People the only creatures with hands, fingers and a thumb capable of grasping?" But as usual their response was flippant and frustrating. "These are irrelevant philosophical questions," the elders said. "But if you must have an answer, it is because the People are created in the Maker's image."

What a shallow and stupid answer Tenge had thought at the time. "How could such basic questions be irrelevant," he asked himself again. "If I can see the World through the eyes of the forest animals, why can't the People see the World through my eyes? Why can't others see the World from my perspective? More mysteries," he sighed. He couldn't help but smile as he saw himself shake his head from the perspective of the forest animals.

He felt the breeze blowing gently on the fine hairs of his muscular neck and this brought him back from his questions and the perspective of the forest animals. "The cooling breeze is wonderful," he thought. The coolness was almost palpable, like the sensation one feels when first drinking cold water and you feel it cool your throat down to your stomach. "Life is good," he concluded, despite its inscrutable mysteries.

"And once again I come full circle in my thoughts," he said aloud to himself. He surprised himself with the impertinence of his vocalization. "Speaking out may not be sophisticated or politically correct, but I like to do it occasionally," he said boldly to himself. "Perhaps we've become too formal and we should lighten up and have some fun shouting or even singing and dancing like the ancients describe in the sacred books." He liked the resonant quality of his voice and the freedom to speak, if only to himself. "It's good to be alive!" he shouted, looking upward and wrapping his arms around his body in a self hug of tactile delight. "It's good to be a part of everything!" he sang to the wind.

CHAPTER 5

Live simply so that others may simply live.
GANDHI

Beta Continent

The high pitched shrieks of animals in the treetops and the intense smells of the wet jungle played across !Kerrt's mind as she stalked in the dim pre-dawn light. It was becoming hard to tell whether the pangs of hunger and the emotions of fear were her own or from her prey. She had been tracking the herd of Ela for several days now and her tension was as great as her need. She knew this band of Ela would be especially dangerous because she sensed several young males among the majority of females and the one dominant male. But she was driven by the desperation that comes from hunger and the realization that she must soon feed or die.

Her strategy was simple, written on the very fabric of her being. It was the timeless struggle of hunter in search of prey. It was kill or, in her case, die of starvation. She hoped her superior senses and hunting experience would be enough to maneuver and isolate a young member at the periphery of the herd and then attack quickly enough to escape with her prize before the herd could turn on her collectively. She knew that she was nearing the limit of her reserves, and she could not afford any mistakes or even delay the attack much longer. It was do or die, success or lingering death with her life forces ebbing away.

Her species of great panther-like creatures had hunted Ela in the forests and across the plains forever, but now there seemed to be fewer of the great herbivores than at any time she could remember. When she wasn't so hungry !Kerrt puzzled over this troubling observation. "Where have all the Ela gone?" she wondered. Her range was extensive so she thought it unlikely that the herds had just migrated away. Also, it seemed that the Ela had become more resourceful defending themselves in recent cycles. And most troubling was that there were now more hunters in her forest range, her territory, than ever before. She frequently sensed their thought patterns as they also hunted the dwindling and only viable supply of food. She had fought these *Others* in limited territorial battles, and in each contact she noted in them the same sense of desperation and puzzlement over the dwindling supply of food that sustained them all. These territorial encounters had often been violent and she had barely escaped serious injury on more than one occasion.

It had now been weeks since her last kill and she knew that the gnawing pangs of hunger lessoned her concentration. She worried that her sensory abilities might also be diminished, but there was nothing she could do about that. Closing her two lower eyes she concentrated and extended her mind outward through her *seeing* eye located at the apex of her triangular face. She could "feel" the troubled thoughts of the herd up wind of her, and she could smell their unmistakable musk through the nasal slits along her muzzle. The herd was at the extreme range of her weakened perceptions, and the background disorganized thoughts coming from the innumerable small forest animals caused problems as she attempted to triangulate the herd. And then with a start she sensed the thoughts of the *Other* who was also moving closer and hunting "her" Ela. "How did he get so near without me sensing him?" she wondered to herself. "I must really be distracted or dangerously weak."

As !Kerrt moved carefully through the jungle darkness, she tried to shut out the thoughts of the tiny life forms scurrying around her four massive clawed feet and those in the forest canopy above. These creatures were of little interest to her. The thought patterns of these small animals were so disorganized that they were of little food value. Occasionally she could glean helpful information about Ela from the unique perspectives of these tiny creatures, but mostly she tried to shut out the cacophony of their primitive thoughts and prevent the noise from intruding on her instinctual hunting skills. "I wonder if Ela ever try to see through the eyes of animals?" she thought to herself and wondered absently why this perspective had never occurred to her before. "This might explain why the Ela have become more resourceful. Food for thought at a later time," she chided herself. "I need to stay focused today and just survive."

Thinking about the tiny creatures brought back a recent disgusting memory. Out of the desperation driven by hunger, she had tried to harvest the neural energy of a handful of these small creatures. But the distasteful morsels she gleaned were just too little and too primitive to be of much value to her. No, she needed the large concentration of organized neural electrical patterns of the more advanced nervous system of an Ela.

As she maneuvered carefully through the dark jungle her sleek jet black hair quietly shed the undergrowth. She managed to stay down wind of the herd, though there was only a minimal breeze in the early morning forest. The brief but heavy rain a short time before dawn had softened her foot falls on the moist undergrowth. Ordinarily she would be excited by the hunt, but she realized that the adrenaline she now felt was driven more by fear. Not from the prospects of battle as much as from the fear of failure and the debility and slow, horrible death that would follow.

And yet, as she stalked a strange new sensation came to her. She suddenly realized that she felt concern for the *Other* male who was stalking her herd of Ela! "This is really crazy," she thought; "I'm in a desperate situation and I'm feeling concern for an *Other* who may kill me outright or take away my Ela and kill me indirectly. What's the matter with me?"

Generally, encounters were very limited between *Others*, who were naturally solitary creatures throughout their long lives. And because *Others* were at the top of the food chain they had no natural enemies except each other. !Kerrt reasoned that as the Ela became evermore scarce, *Others* were being forced into closer contact with each other making things increasingly dangerous. And yet, she actually felt a kindred experience with this male *Other* who was also stalking the herd. She didn't think this strange empathy was a good thing, given the inherent danger of contact with her kind, even under the best of circumstances. And these were not the best of times.

!Kerrt could sense the same desperation in his mind. And she could feel his hunger. His thoughts betrayed him; he was as depleted and weakened as she was. Unfortunately, she knew that if she could read his thoughts, he could do likewise. She saw that he was new to this coastal forest valley. And she also noted that his thought pattern was… a little different than the *Others* she had skirmished with in recent cycles. But she also knew that this male, although weakened by hunger, would be driven by desperation that would make him even more dangerous.

If we aid each other rather than fighting, there will be enough for both of us, came the startling and intrusive thought in her mind. The power of the projection was striking and almost caused her head to snap backwards from the intensity. There was no doubt in !Kirrt's mind that the male was the source of this communication. But the audacity of his contact shocked her. Was he so close that he could project himself into her mind so powerfully and so brazenly despite her defenses?

She shot back with all the power she could muster. *Do you think me a fool that I would lower my guard and trust you? All you want is to get close enough to attack me or take my Ela! You would love to kill me and then sink your feeding tongue into my Ela!* she sneered.

Believe what you want, female, but you should be able to see through any deception because of our closeness. I do know that the herd we both need has many powerful adults and the attack will be dangerous. Both of us are dangerously weak and it's probable that one of us will die if we fail in our hunt today or if we waste our energies attacking each other. If we can cooperate then we might be successful and then we can go our separate ways.

You are lying, male! she responded with a leer that she hoped was sufficiently threatening. *You just want my Ela and you will stoop to any trick to get me out of the way. Besides, I think you are bluffing because I sense that your energy reserves are so low that I don't believe you could even generate a stun pulse that could harm me,* snapped !Kerrt.

You may be right, female, but I'm larger than you are, and can you take the risk? You and I both know that neither of us has the power to fight each other and attack the herd, responded the male. *By fighting me you will lose the opportunity to attack the Ela today and you may sustain enough injury that your energy-depleted body can't repair. Look into my thoughts, female; see the truth of the situation!* reasoned the male.

!Kerrt was surprised by the clarity of his logic. And she reluctantly concluded that he might be right. It was too big a gamble to fight the male. It was also true that one or both of them would probably die unless they fed soon. She suddenly thought to herself, "How bizarre that I now see cooperation as an option!" She was shocked by her reaction. Ordinarily, she would never even consider working with an *Other.* She thought to herself, "Could this male be exerting some influence on my thinking?" As she thought about the situation she had the queer sensation of being outside herself, watching herself from a vantage point.

She shook herself and refocused, as desperation forced her response. *You're very persuasive and perhaps you're right. But I don't trust you. I am willing to listen. Where are you, and what do you call yourself?*

I call myself !Zsakk. If you refocus your mind you'll see that I'm only about thirty meters southeast of you.

!Kerrt knew he must be close, but she almost panicked when she realized how close he actually was to her. She thought to herself, "How did he get so close without me sensing him?" Rarely did *Others* get close to one another. The only exception was during the infrequent mating times when fertilizing scent-pheromones were passed.

She studied the male as he slowly approached her position, moving quietly through the dense underbrush. *That's close enough, male,* she threatened, at the same time baring her teeth menacingly. *Don't come any closer or I'll kill you!* she growled with as much malice as she could muster.

Cut the crap, female, I know you're bluffing. Now this is the way I see things. We're both downwind of the herd and I believe we can move them toward a natural gorge ahead by playing upon their fears with our thoughts. When the herd moves into the gorge they'll be unable to maneuver as easily as we can and they'll be less able to close ranks and defend the smaller and weaker ones.

!Kerrt instantly saw the logic and the simplicity of the male's plan. Their telepathic skills could be used in concert to confuse and misdirect the herd and maneuver them to the hunters' advantage. She had used her telepathic skills to find and track Ela, usually by seeing the terrain through their mind's eyes. But it had never occurred to her to use her skills to manipulate an Ela's mind! Why had she never thought of such a tactic? It seemed so logical after the male's suggestion. And to work in a hunt with an *Other* was also novel, and very dangerous. Her hunger and desperation must be what was driving her to risk so much and even consider such a liaison. Was hunger also affecting her judgment? Was she reading his thoughts and intentions correctly? Would he kill her if she trusted him and let her guard down? But there didn't seem to be any other solution. She would have to trust her instincts and proceed with this drastic plan.

She shot back, *Where did you get the idea of manipulating the mind of the herd?*

I really don't know. It just came to me as we both stalked the herd and became aware of each other. It suddenly just seemed logical to use both our minds together. Listen female, I'm as disgusted as you are by the thought of working together, growled !Zsakk.

She thought about his words and then with as much pride as she could muster, *Well, how can I trust you not to attack me?*

If I wanted to attack you we wouldn't be having this discussion. Think about it, female. Could I fool you, given that we are so close and our thoughts are so entwined? Look into my mind, woman! To prove my sincerity, I'll lower the last shields protecting my mind. I'm the one risking attack by opening myself up to you.

!Kerrt saw his shields go down and she probed his mind marveling at his courage to bare himself to her. She could detect no duplicity. It was true that she could attack his mind now, and injure him, but she probably couldn't destroy him, and given his closeness, he would undoubtedly counter attack with a fury and perhaps injure her seriously.

Pulling back from the depths of his mind she asked, *Have you ever worked with an Other like this before?*

Never! came the almost instantaneous and indignant reply. *As I told you, I find our interaction disgusting, even though my gut sense tells me that it is necessary for me to survive.*

You are a very interesting creature, !Zsakk. I've never encountered one like you before. If we survive each other and if we're successful in this hunt, then perhaps we can think about what has happened here between us. But right now that's too many ifs and I'm too hungry to worry or to think anymore. Let's hunt, survive the day and then we'll see what's next. By the way, my name is !Kerrt.

CHAPTER 6

We had the sky, up there, all speckled with stars, and we used
to lay [sic] on our backs and look up at them, and discuss about
whether they was [sic] made, or only just happened.

MARK TWAIN from
Huckleberry Finn

"Wait up, Doc," called Xenobiologist Linda Wade as she ran the last
few steps and jumped onto the lift with Chief Medical Officer Helen
Tapp. The somewhat cramped lift softly resumed its journey down-
ship carrying them from their dormitory floor and jump stations to
the Science deck.

Tapp nodded to her room mate and smiled inwardly at Wade's
perpetually frenzied persona now fueled by the general excitement in
the ship. Everyone felt the growing anticipation now permeating the
ship after the Captain's announcement that they were moving toward
an orbital insertion of the planet referred to as G38-2. To the ever
observant doctor the excitement was justifiable and more intense in
those crewmembers whose expertise would be necessary for orbital
operations or a planetary landing and exploration. But Tapp sensed
the electric atmosphere even in the engineering crew, whom everyone
kiddingly referred to as the grease monkeys, though Tapp had never
seen any grease in the spotless rooms housing the ship's nuclear power
plant.

Locking her right hand in the wall strap, Tapp reflected on
her observations of the crew and the buzz that she sensed as almost

palpable. This was after all what most of them had signed on for, but now it became more real as they approached an alien world. The quiet hum of the elevator and her thoughts were quickly interrupted by her youthful and effervescent roommate, who could scarcely contain her excitement.

As the gate closed behind her Wade blurted out, "Doc, I'm just praying this planet justifies a landing! It kills me to get so close to a new world and still be so far away. I've just got to get off this ship and down on a planet! Everyone else can do some type of useful work from a distance or even from an orbit; but I can't do anything from space."

Tapp surveyed the young biologist and forced herself to just listen. Too often she found herself responding and trying to fix things. After years of trying to fix problems she was more and more trying to just lend a sympathetic ear. It was amazing that people seemed to find a solution to their questions if given space to think out loud or ventilate.

Tapp just held on as Wade shifted to a new beef without a break or even slowing her banter. "And have you talked to the Captain about lifting the requirements that everyone strap down every time we jump? We've gone through dozens of jumps now and it's getting to be a real pain in the ass to stop everything and *buckle up*."

Tapp studied the young biologist who seemed so full of herself and so full of energy. "Ah, to have this much energy again," mused Tapp to herself. But Wade was, in one sense, like all the crew; they were somewhat younger than Tapp was. "I used to be so young and bubbly and...fearless, not so long ago," she remembered, all the while listening to her protégé. Tapp managed to get an answer in among Wade's monologue as the young scientist paused for a breath. "I know everyone is bitching about the Captain's regulations. But in his defense, jumping, or should I say "falling" through some damn wormhole, remains tricky business. No one really understands what happens to our parts when we strap ourselves down and enter a reality that we were never designed for." She didn't tell Wade about the nightmare she had several nights ago. Tapp's analysis of her dream was related to free-fall through a wormhole. The vision of her organs rotating like a chicken on a spit was still vivid in her mind.

Tapp continued. "It's true; we haven't found any problems jumping around all over space and sub-space. Since you and everyone else are complaining to me all the time about this requirement, I'll mention it again to the Captain and see if we can get the regulation lifted by the time we leave this system."

"Thanks, Doc. I'm sure you'll get stars in your crown if you can get the Captain to lighten up. I just hope that this planet is as favorable as everyone seems to think. I'm itching to get off the ship and my get hands in some alien dirt!"

Sometimes Tapp felt like she just had to hold on tightly to something as her frenetic suite mate again shifted topics without any obvious segue. In one sense Tapp sympathized with her roommate. Xenobiology was the study of alien biological systems and could realistically only be done on an alien planet. Wade's field was a relatively new branch of biology and was only created when humankind expanded to the planets of the Sol system. But now all the planets and even the moons of the home system had been thoroughly studied. Xenobiologists like Linda needed to go to the stars to make their mark and their careers.

"Linda, I have to tell you that I think it's a bit disgusting to imagine you making alien mud patties, but I realize you're just kidding about the dirt thing. I do wish that everyone on this ship would take a deep breath and slow down," said Tapp. "We're all excited, but a lot of work needs to be done before any planet-fall is considered. I'm sure you'll be critical of this cautious attitude, but it still concerns me that the bio-filters are, in my opinion, a technology that's still too new to be taken for granted."

Tapp held up her hand as Wade began to interrupt her *lecture of caution*. "Don't panic, Linda. You'll eventually get your wish and get your feet in the mud of some damn planet! I just hope our technology is up to the task to protect you. Listen kid, you need to take things slowly. Remember Tapp's rule number one: 'It's bad enough to get sick, it's worse to be sick fifty light-years from home.'"

"I know, I know," said the younger scientist with a poorly disguised air of exasperation. "I do listen to you, Helen. Hell, you have more experience than almost anyone else on this ship," admitted Wade. "But you have to admit the bio-filters have worked perfectly on all the other planets we've explored. Now don't get me wrong; I'm all in favor of some caution. But there are just some risks in what we do; especially what I do, what I need to do! I just have to have faith that our technology will keep me safe and that you'll save my butt if I run into some 'Andromeda strain' on G38-2."

"Yeah, I hope our technology is up to the task," said Tapp wistfully. "It's just that the complexities of this entire undertaking almost overwhelm me at times. We all know the risks and, yes, we have to take chances; the very fact that we are on this ship is a leap of faith," exclaimed Tapp. "Think about it, Linda. We travel across unimaginable distances through other dimensions, and now we propose to slog around on a planet that our immune systems have never even dreamed of! And I'm not sure if I'll ever get used to the things the jump engines do to my atoms and my stomach. But here I am among you 'spacemen' trying to impart a word of caution."

"And we love ya, Doc, ole venerable one!" joked Wade. "And we even love the canned lectures that you can pull out at the drop of a hat!"

"Now that really hurts, Linda," feigned Tapp. "I know I'm *old* by comparison to most of you, but not by that damn much! I'm only 38, so give me a break."

"Hey, you know I'm just kidding, Helen. Do the jump engines really bother you? You know, I kind of like the sensation we get when we jump," quipped Wade. "The tingling of the hairs on the back of my neck and arms from the warp field generators and then the sensation of falling just as we enter the event horizon of the wormhole reminds me of the Triple Demon ride at the Portland World's Fair!"

Tapp grimaced as she recalled similar youthful memories of amusement park rides. She could barely tolerate the free-fall simulators used in her pre-flight training. She only survived these encounters by concentration and telling herself, "It's really not the free-fall of space, Helen," even as the floor fell away from her and her stomach welled up into her throat.

"Well, that's one real difference between us," said Tapp. "As a kid, the only *rush* I felt in an amusement ride was nausea. Being turned upside down and inside out is not my idea of a good time."

Wade and Tapp had had many discussions of each other's philosophy of adventure and risk taking as they lay awake at night at the end of their watches. Though age engendered a difference between them regarding risk taking and mortality, Wade and all the crew realized that they were dependant on the expertise and advice of all the specialties on the ship, not the least of these was the ship's medical staff. Wade knew she would be at particular risk from a planetary contagion, as would any other member of the ship's company who was part of a landing team. Wade couldn't help but look with morbid curiosity at some of the terrible pictures in Tapp's medical data base. She certainly didn't want to "get some exotic fungus on the tip of my nose!"

Wade had gone over the risks dozens of times before she ever accepted the posting to *Odyssey*. But the Doctor's cautions made her stop and weigh the risks again. And this was good, she thought. The balance between caution and risk-taking had been drummed into all of them in mission preparations, "but it never hurts to hear it again, I guess." And the opportunity to go with *Odyssey* was the chance of a lifetime. "Hell's bells," she chided herself. "I'm damned lucky to be a part of something so important."

Wade stiffened her resolve and shrugged off her apprehensions. "Keep reminding me of reality, Doc, but I'm convinced that I'm doing what I'm supposed to be doing with my life. I'm not fatalistic, but I'm committed now, and certain aspects of the mission depend on me. I just can't allow myself to dwell on the possibilities. I need to stay focused on the probabilities."

"Well said, Linda." But despite her bravado Tapp could sense Linda's doubts, even though it wasn't *cool* to voice them. But she had to admire Wade's courage, her sense of responsibility and her ability to manage her fears. "She was truly the liberated woman," Tapp thought to herself.

The lift approached the science deck. "Doc, I hope you'll want to work with my team as we study G38-2. We'd even be glad to have you go planet-side with us if there's a landing."

"Oh no!" said Tapp, shaking her head with conviction. "I'm happy to advise your team, but there's no way I'm going down to the planet. The Captain and I discussed this long ago. I can best serve in

41

a back up role and let you *young Turks* go down to the planet. Besides, someone will need to be here to bring you a bed pan if you get sick!"

"Ooh.., that's a disturbing thought," said Wade, pursing her lips like a prune as she considered the vision of her backside perched atop a bedpan.

Wade quickly changed the subject, "I've been reading your research paper on evolutionary brain development. It's really quite fascinating. Who knows, if we find life on the second planet you may get additional support for your theory of comparative development and you'll be famous!"

As the lift arrived on the science deck, Tapp managed only a half hearted reply of "maybe." She briefly thought about the work she and her team had published just before *Odyssey's* departure. Her research team had demonstrated the ability to enhance neuronal dendritic connections in the brains of primates when stimulated by a graviton field. The question she and her group were exploring was whether selective adjustments of these neural connections, especially in the frontal and temporal lobes of the brain, could augment functional capabilities. It may have been a stretch, but they had speculated on the possibility of developing extreme empathic skills or even telepathic abilities.

She had met with her research team before she left and shared with them her wildest dreams for their research. "This could end up as a real breakthrough for mankind; the next evolutionary jump for humanity. Imagine communication by telepathy. We might even be able to communicate with chimps and dolphins! But there is at least one downside," she half joked. "If the research pans out, it will ruin Vegas and the video poker network. There won't be anymore bluffing!" she laughed.

So her decision to accept the Chief Medical Officer position on *Odyssey* had been an agonizing one. It meant that others would take the lead in her work on Earth and they would be the ones exploring these exciting possibilities. And now every time the jump engines *torqued* her body, she wondered if she had made the right decision. But she really admired Captain Havel; and his arguments had been good ones. She would only be gone three to six months and she wasn't too old to challenge herself. It was his comment about getting old that was the straw that broke her reluctance. As she studied herself in the mirror the next morning she made up her mind as she told herself with as much conviction as she could muster that "I'm not too old!" And so here she was, out of the lab, out of her comfort zone and out among the stars. "*Stars* like this kid," she admitted to herself as she studied Wade. "If this kid can be so bold, so can I," she nodded with resolve. Tapp had to admit that it was energizing to be a part of the competitive spirit she'd observed in all the crew. The challenge was like her residency training and was downright *infectious*.

"And besides, it's too late to turn back now," she muttered as the lift door opened and she stepped out onto deck fourteen.

CHAPTER 7

If I have seen farther than other men, it is because I have stood on the shoulders of giants.
ISAAC NEWTON

By the 23rd century the complexities of interplanetary flight and orbital insertion had become more or less a routine maneuver. And after more than a century of interplanetary flights to Mars and the outer planets of the Sol systems, ion drive systems had become very efficient and required relatively little reaction mass. The only problem was that *Odyssey* had a finite supply of hydrogen that served as the reactant for the ion drive and therefore conservation was a necessity.

Havel watched his pilot chase the navigational bubble on the flight board down to their final geo-synchronous orbit above the 2nd planet. He and his Exec had chosen a stationary orbit above the largest of the two landmasses on the mostly water world of G38-2. The data on their approach to the planet had become increasingly favorable over the last twenty four hours. The oxygen content of the planet's atmosphere as well as the ambient temperatures bode well for the possibility of life-forms, even earth-like ones.

The excitement of the crew was "palpable," as the good Dr. Tapp had described in the officer's mess last watch. Havel enjoyed watching Hinton roll his eyes at Tapp's medical lingo, that she called "medical-eze". Havel kidded him, "Come on, Steve, haven't you ever referred to a common place occurrence in tech-terms? Actually, I think

I can *feel* the mood of the crew. Everyone is so excited about this new planet, even us." Though he didn't discuss this with the officers, Havel's big concern was maintaining a professional attitude on the flight deck, especially his.

"Stable orbit achieved, Captain," reported his chief pilot, Ensign Joanna Wise.

She is truly a whiz kid thought Havel. There was never any doubt in her demeanor as she deftly maneuvered the huge ship with her joystick like a home entertainment game. On completion of the maneuver she switched to the autopilot to maintain a station-keeping attitude. He observed her work with appreciation. "We never waste any drive mass when Joanna is in the driver's seat."

Havel knew that Joanna had overcome so much to finally get her chance and use what he recognized as a gift. She was not from the academy, as were most of the bridge crew. Getting her a slot on *Odyssey* had been a real uphill battle. But Havel felt strongly that it was best to match a person's natural talents with their passions. Putting a person in a critical job because of rank or academic credentials might work in some situations, but not fifty light-years from Earth. Many had questioned his decision to choose Wise as his pilot, but her experience flying interplanetary shuttles and transports was second to none. Havel personally saw her gift for spatial arrangements one day as she was forced to dock a shuttle with an orbital space station when the autopilot failed. Her deft feel was evident to Havel and all those on board the malfunctioning boat as she flawlessly executed the tricky maneuver. Havel had put her up for a commendation and argued for a promotion that would give her a chance to advance. But it was Joanna's skill that eventually won over even the skeptics in the numerous training simulations and shakedown runs prior to *Odyssey*'s official launch.

"Thank you, Pilot. Good job, again. Mr. Hinton, notify all the science labs that we will be studying the land mass designated as Alpha for the next twenty four hours and then we'll change our position to study the Beta landmass. I want a list of potential landing sites on both continents, in addition to the usual geophysical and cartographical surveys.

Turning on the ship's intercom Havel spoke to the crew. "Listen up, people, this is the Captain speaking. I know everyone is excited about this planet. The best thing any of you can do is buckle down and get the survey work done. Your job is to find me a reason to go down to the surface. Havel out!"

"Mr. Hinton, have Astrophysicist Emily Blair meet me in stellar cartography. You have the bridge, Steve."

Aye, Sir."

Havel needed to get off the bridge and out of the way of his people. It was hard for him to let them do their work. And he was also afraid they would see how antsy he was. A captain needed to maintain the appearance of calm and that he was in control of the situation and himself. But he was so excited that it was difficult to appear calm. And he didn't have a specific job at this moment. So he decided to busy himself with a ship's status issue. More importantly, he hadn't met with his chief astrophysicist Emily Blair in a number of weeks. He secretly hoped he would get there before Dr. Blair, giving him the opportunity to play with her holographic star chamber. It was the closest he ever came to playing a video game.

He took the bridge lift down two decks to the stellar cartography room and was excited to see that Dr. Blair hadn't arrived yet. He always felt like a kid on his first visit to a planetarium, sitting in the darkened room with the real time computer images of the local and distant stars swirling around him in the holographic display. The computer oriented the stars in such a way as to put *Odyssey* and G38 at the center of the hologram. His vision swept over the stars they had recently visited. He could follow their path back across space and time to Sol and to home. He thought of Becky. "We're so far away, my love. I hope you know that I'm thinking of you," he murmured to the small yellow orb that represented the Sol star system.

"Captain...?" a voice from behind him trailed off on an expectant note.

"Come in, Dr. Blair. I just love to sit and play with your hologram. It helps me to appreciate the big picture. I needed to get off the bridge and I wanted us to do a little planning. I'd like your opinion on a few things."

"I'm glad you're here, Captain, and I'm really glad that you have an interest in my department. This ship is so big, and I know you're pulled in many directions. I love this place too, probably even more than you do. Please call me, Emily, Captain.

"Ok, Emily, please update me on our position and status."

"Well Captain, you can see where we are now," as she pointed with a red laser light. "And this is where we've been." Blair traced their course backward, showing each of the nine star systems they had visited since leaving the home system. "Our course is displayed by the faint yellow line, and the distances to the local stars and to Sol are listed beneath each star. The alphabetic letter beneath each star describes the star type. As you know we are primarily interested in G and K star types, as these are the ones closest to Sol in configuration and energy output. The numbers and the X's, between G37 and our current location, are our jump coordinates. Our last jump was approximately seven parsecs, a record I think, Sir."

"Yes, I guess 21 light-years is a record, unless *Pegasus* is out here somewhere setting records of her own," Havel replied.

"Well, we won't know about that till we get home," said Blair waving her laser baton like a conductor. "As you can see, Captain, *Pegasus*' planned survey route was outward and away from Galactic center along the Orion spiral. I don't mean to be condescending, Sir, but that's the spiral arm of the Milky Way where our home is. As you can also see our route was inward along the Orion spiral toward the Galaxy's center. I believe we have done well these last two months, Sir. Several of the planets we've scouted will be worth closer inspection on future missions."

"Yes, I suppose they will. But I'm interested in two things right now. I want you to start thinking about where we will go next. As you know we are about half way through our mission and I want to survey as many G type stars as possible before we turn for home."

"I understand, Sir. I've been thinking about this, but some of my recommendations will depend on how long we stay here. I'll work on several scenarios based on one or two weeks in this system. Do you think we might stay here even longer, Sir?"

"I don't really know, Emily, but I doubt it. A lot depends on whether we land on the planet below us. What can you tell me about this star, this planet's orbit, and the possibility of life on G38-2, at least life as we understand?"

"Well, Sir, as we discussed a few weeks ago, this star looked quite promising from our distant survey. I've looked at the data repeatedly as we made the several jumps to get to this system. I've also reviewed the data as we approached orbit. I've spoken with many of the other scientists as well. Everything looks very favorable as far as Earth-like conditions and life. But don't get your hopes up. As you know this is the thirty-eighth G or K type star system humans have encountered, and though we have found some primitive life forms, we haven't found anything much more interesting. Perhaps others may dispute my speculations, but we still seem to be alone in the universe."

"Yes, so it seems," said Havel wistfully under his breath.

Blair noted the Captain's demeanor and knew of his hopes of finding thoughtful life. "On the other hand I wouldn't be too discouraged, Sir. Back in the late twentieth century a man named Frank Drake wrote an equation theorizing the likelihood of sentient life in the universe given the number of suns like ours. Given the four hundred billion stars in our galaxy alone, he calculated that there must be millions of advanced civilizations. The problem is the vastness of space. Another guy somewhat later, I believe his name was Carl Sagan, estimated that these same hypothetical civilizations would be on the average two hundred light-years apart. As you know, Sir, we've traveled a great distance, but fifty light-years is nothing in the vastness of the Milky Way or the universe."

"Yes, I see your point; and it's one that I need to be reminded of occasionally. Thanks for your perspective. It helps. And thanks for letting me play with your Game Boy. I had a lot of fun and I think it's important for the Captain to have a little fun occasionally. But please don't tell anyone I was down here fooling around.

"You're welcome here any time, Captain, and your secret is safe, Sir."

"Make your travel plans, Emily. We have a galaxy to explore and I don't believe we'll be here more than a few days."

CHAPTER 3

My suspicion is that the Universe is not only [stranger] than we
suppose,but [stranger] than we can suppose.
JOHN HALDANE

The energy-being Quixt continued to analyze the aliens as he followed
their starship to Tenge's *World*. He liked this quaint and encompassing
term used by the *People* to describe their planet and all they knew.
Only Tenge seemed remotely capable of imagining something beyond
the horizon or across the sea. But to these star travelers the *World* was
just another promising planet to visit. "Amazing how one's perspective
changes things," he thought. "One person's world is another's afternoon
excursion." Quixt might have shaken his head, if he had had one, as
he considered the conundrum before him. Waxing philosophically, he
thought, "The interloper's designation of G38-2 really does seem so
inadequate to describe such a jewel of a planet that floats below us in
the utter blackness of space."

Quixt's initial concerns about the newcomers were now long
since gone. His scans of their main computer showed that they were
not conquerors. Even greater assurances came as he gently touched
the minds of the crew. He didn't think he could be shocked again,
but as he probed them, Quixt came upon the startling revelation that
these aliens were the decendants of his "shepherds" on ancient and
far away Earth! He was so startled that he was forced to draw back
and disconnect his probe for fear that he might be detected. He then
dampened his surging energy screen as he considered the staggering

coincidence before him! He almost thought out loud, "Who could have imagined that the Terrans, who now call themselves humans, could advance so rapidly and would show up in the same system where I'm working?" It seemed too incredible that their arrival at this time and place could be mere chance. "Serendipity among the stars?" he wondered. "Why, the odds of such an occurrence are unimaginable. But what could explain this?" he asked himself. "The only logical explanation is this is the Lord's work!" Quixt focused his mind and challenged the darkness. *If my analysis is faulty, correct me!* He waited, but didn't really expect an answer. However, "sometimes no response is an answer in and of itself," he "smiled" wistfully to himself.

He marveled at how far "his Terrans" had come! In a mere twelve thousand years they had advanced from shepherding to developing a technology to bridge the vast gulf between the stars. Quixt forced himself to stifle a sense of pride of his accomplishment. "Steady now, ole boy; don't you forget who is really in charge here," he chided himself. "This is but a part of the Great Design."

The accomplishments of the Terrans made Quixt reconsider the issue of interstellar travel. "Perhaps you place the stars so far apart to keep species away from each, at least until they are ready," he thought to himself and half heartedly to the Progenitor. *Are you listening?* He quickly admonished himself with a prayer into the void, *Forgive me, Lord. I again fall short in my faith. If this is indeed your Design, then it is wondrous and...sublime!*

Bowing his "heart" he projected his thoughts into the void. *Progenitor, I wish that sometime I could get a sign, some validation of my work and the direction of my labors. I know that I've asked this of you before, but I ask again. This coming rendezvous of Terrans, the People, and Others is just too confusing. Are you behind this meeting? Tell me if I am doing the right thing.*

But again there was no answer from the darkness; and then the mind games within him resumed. "Am I kidding myself?" he wondered. "Are we *Quixt* deluding ourselves as we work? Is our service and allegiance to an ideal merely filling our own need to be a part of something greater?"

He suddenly became aware of a peculiar sensation, experienced as an unusual sparking energy pattern that played over his neural net, like electricity off a Van de Graph generator. "I'm lonely!" he realized with a shock. He had never experienced this reaction before. He thought, "The *People* are connected to each other, and the Terrans are likewise interdependent, but I have no one except perhaps the distant *Quixt* and the silent void." And for the first time in his existence he recognized what could best be described as self pity. He shuddered at the thought of only an existential existence without a purpose or the Designer.

He shook himself, halting the pattern of circular logic that always ended with his return to the wonders around him. With a humbled heart he bowed: *Forgive me, Progenitor, my Lord. I am not alone. I am part of the Design,* he cried out again to the void. *How could I deny my changed nature or the majesty of the universe around me? How could I argue the improbability of a random universe or the improbable arrival of the Terrans? No, the most likely explanation for all these events is that everything is Your work. And the Terrans' arrival is the assurance that I've sought for so long. Every sentient creature that I've ever helped has moments of doubt, Lord. I guess I am no different.*

Although adrenaline no longer flowed in Quixt, the templates for such primeval emotions persisted at a different level and now surged across his energy matrix as he considered how blessed he was. He was a part of the Great Design, the great dance of life. He became aware of his passion and again moved to dampen the fluxing energies of epiphanal joy so as not to be detected by the Terran sensors. He scolded himself for another lapse into doubt and then self-indulgent pride. "How many times do I have to stumble before doubt is erased?" he asked himself the age-old question again.

"Enough questions, Mr. Quixt, and enough speculation," he chided himself. "You need to stay focused on your job and leave the rest to the Designer. Now, get back to work and have some faith. Things will sort themselves out."

Quixt returned to duty and analysis of the Terrans whose starship now hung beside him in orbit. He could see the templates he had fashioned so long ago, still evident in the Terran's genomic DNA. Quixt marveled at "how much of me is in them." *We both seem to have an engram that urges us to search for relationship with you, my Lord. Did you or one of your agents plant this matrix in me and the Quixt? Are there other aspects of you in me, Lord?*

Quixt reflected on his work with the *People* who seemed to be stuck in a developmental plateau. "Perhaps this unforeseen arrival of the Terrans is just what they need. Perhaps they need a kick in the proverbial pants and meeting the Terrans will do just that. Maybe this will do what I've been unable to do. And admit it, Quixt, you don't have a clue of what to do with the *Others*, even though they were originally as promising as the *People*." *Progenitor, maybe you know that I need help, and this rendezvous is just what the doctor ordered!* "And maybe, just maybe, the Terrans will get a kick in their *spiritual pants* as well," he laughed to himself.

Quixt knew the Terrans to be a technology based culture and this power had dangers. He had seen knowledge and advances in science erode a culture's sense of the sacred many times in his travels. Sadly some cultures lost the appreciation of mystery, replacing it with false gods. He thought, "Wisdom really comes when you understand that you can't know and master everything. Maybe it's the recognition of one's limits that opens the way to enlightenment," he speculated. Quixt saw that the Terrans had not encountered thoughtful, sentient life forms yet. "So perhaps the shock of contact will be a wake up call to the Terran's hubris as well."

Quixt's desire to make himself known to the Terrans was intense, but he held back. He kept reminding himself that this was not his primary focus. And by meddling he would undoubtedly add even more uncertainty to an already complicated situation. "And what would you say to them, Quixt, if you did pop in on them? 'Hello, I am Quixt. I am an energy being who altered your brains and helped your ancestors evolve to a higher level of thoughtfulness thousands of years ago.' Yeah, sure, that would go over well!" He could picture the chaotic scene, with the Terran's faces contorted in horror and disgust, if not disbelief. "No, I don't need to 'pop in' and add even greater complexities to a stew that is already about to boil over."

CHAPTER 9

People almost invariably arrive at their beliefs, not on the basis of
proof, but on the basis of what they find attractive.

BLAISE PASCAL

Alpha Continent

It had been twelve great-cycles since Tenge had first looked up
at the stars with a new sense of wonder and curiosity about his place
in the World and the World's place among the lights of the night. He
still remembered the place in his field when he first had the notion of
"other places," ones even beyond the horizon. He remembered how
odd the insight had seemed to him at the time, and yet so obvious to
him afterwards. He thought about these things mostly in private now
because no one else seemed interested in his passion or, for that matter,
seemed capable of thinking beyond the horizon.

He and Kitu's bonding had culminated in a wondrous creation
of their love, a child. This little one had brought to Tenge an even
deeper sense of connection to life's cycle and a greater appreciation
for the Maker of all things. He now saw the Maker as not only the
creator of the World, but of new life, and all the other places he had
imagined, even the lights in the night sky. The Villagers and Kitu saw
the Maker in much more simplistic ways, but it didn't matter. Tenge
pictured the love that he shared with Kitu as just another manifestation
of the Maker, shining through to the here and now. And the Maker's

wonderful gift of love now encompassed their little one as well. He felt such peace in his heart and the rightness of his life.

The shamans said that a man was right with the Maker when his crops were successful and his family was blessed with children. "If this is the measure of a man then I must be right with the Maker," he dared to think. But he worried about those who were not so blessed. Were they not right with the Maker? Were they being punished as the shamans suggested? He couldn't believe this and often debated this perspective with others in his Village, including the Elders. And he didn't agree with the Village wisdom that illness or bad weather or a failed crop was a result of the Maker's anger for some overt or subtle sin. But life went on and was good. He didn't have all the answers, but that was all right. He knew and experienced the really important aspects of life.

They named their child Roosa, meaning that which comes of love. All parents feel that their children are special, but it was apparent to Tenge and Kitu that their Roosa was more than just precocious. During her pregnancy Kitu had confided to him that she sensed Roosa's mind, though never a specific thought. This had obviously concerned him, but he had passed it off as a mother's intuition, especially since this was Kitu's first pregnancy. But when Roosa was born even Tenge felt the child's mind! He recalled being afraid and prayed that the old woman helping Kitu with the birth wouldn't sense the child's mind. Reading the thoughts of others was not supposed to happen until a child's Awakening. But if the old woman sensed anything she said nothing, and as time went by Tenge and Kitu felt that their secret was safe.

As Roosa grew so did the power of her mind. There was never an open conversation between parents and child, but there were brief glimpses of something powerful just under the surface of perception. Fortunately, no one else seemed to be aware of Roosa's precocity. Tenge and Kitu remained fearful that Roosa's gift might be misinterpreted by the superstitious villagers as evil. Fortunately, even Roosa's grandparents were oblivious to the child's agile mind.

All parents want the best for their children and want them to excel, though not to be seen as excessively different from other children. Tenge had to admit that Roosa had been the best baby and she was the sweetest child he had ever been around. It was as though all living things were drawn to her, especially birds and forest animals, which seemed unafraid around her. And her interaction with other children and villagers was remarkable at every age.

Time takes care of a lot of things, and though Tenge and Kitu continued to be concerned about Roosa, she would soon go through the Awakening and they wouldn't have to carry the secret any longer. All they had to do was shelter their daughter a little longer and they would all be home free.

As he moved out of the Village toward his fields, Tenge saw the fading lights of the night. He pondered their beauty and their mystery. He thought, "Could these points of light be other suns that were just very far away?" He almost stumbled at the audacity of his thought. And by extension, "Could there be other worlds, other places near these suns like my World? Where do these thoughts come from?" he wondered. "Maybe Kitu is right; maybe I am crazy to have such thoughts."

He certainly had no formal education. His village was very small and education was mostly for men, primarily to help them read the sacred scrolls. And yet thoughts came into his mind, and somehow it seemed important to him to explore the thought line. Even if it was just a dream, he enjoyed thinking about the possibilities as he loped along, "It's really quite strange that no one else wonders about the lights of the night sky. I wonder what makes me have these thoughts."

The bright flash low in the pre-dawn sky to the northeast was followed several seconds later by a distant rumble of "thunder." His reflections were rudely interrupted, and if he hadn't been looking at the morning lights, he might have missed the flash or mistaken the thunder for a distant spring storm. As a light-gazer, he knew instantly that this was not a "falling light" or even a spring storm. This flash and thunder were different. Scanning the sky in the direction of the noise, he saw a thin line of streaking light and could just make out an object low on the horizon against the growing light of dawn. Whatever it was the thing appeared to lose speed and then it dropped straight down from the sky several leagues away. He looked around, but there was no one else on the road with him. He knew that it was unlikely that any other villager would have seen this phenomenon. His land was farther east of the Village than the other farms and the others did not study the sky as he did.

"What should I do?" he almost thought out loud as he considered his options. Should he go and try to get other villagers so they could all go and explore the mystery? He rapidly decided that they wouldn't see any reason to waste time trying to solve such a mystery. And they would probably just kid him again. Should he just ignore the flash in the sky? He decided that the unresolved mystery would really drive him crazy. No, he'd have to go alone and solve the mystery himself. Farming would just have to wait for another day.

He estimated that the object had come down on the other side of the coastal forest that circled the nearby ocean bay. It would probably take one third of a cycle to reach the general area. He could easily be back by sundown and no one would even know that he was gone or criticize him for wasting time and daydreaming. He had no fear, only a sense of excitement. He had to go, he told himself; his curiosity was like an itch that had to be scratched. And before he knew what was happening, his running legs were carrying him toward the horizon and toward adventure!

As he turned to the northeast, he lengthened the stride of his running legs. He easily found a rhythm and began to enjoy his efforts. "This is a lot better than digging in the dirt," he smiled to himself. He felt like a school boy playing hooky from work to go fishing. As he bounded along, the wind sang in his long elliptical ears. He angled them backward to avoid the steady roar from the wind and to protect the delicate inner surfaces from the branches of trees and the underbrush. Somehow he felt more alive now than he had in some time. "I'm doing something completely out of the ordinary and it feels good!" It was as if all the years of containing his passions had been loosened in the quest of something mysterious, something wondrous.

He moved along the ocean bay and quickly rose ever higher above the level of the sea. There were no further unusual sounds or lights during his journey. He detected nothing unusual in the minds of the animals as he flushed them and sent them scurrying into the bush. By angling slightly north away from the sea line, he knew he could stay mostly in the forest until he reached the peninsula's base.

It was easy going and he knew the forest trails quite well. He and others from the Village often traveled this route when journeying to neighboring villages at festival times. He remembered a large area of grassland that rose slowly toward the coastal mountains. It seemed to him to be about the spot where the object fell. As he loped along his mind played over the possibilities. "Maybe I'm crazy to be doing this. Kitu will be really disappointed if she finds out that I wasted a whole day chasing dreams. But a man has to have some passion, doesn't he? This adventure, or what ever it turns out to be, is exciting; I won't deny that. I love my wife and my life, but I've just got to do this," he convinced himself.

He refreshed himself from a stream and thought about trying to catch a fish for a meal, but he decided to make do with the lunch Kitu had given him that morning. "Besides I'm too excited to be very hungry."

He continued on quickly and soon approached the upland meadow he sought. As he moved through the forest he reached out with his mind toward the flying sea birds to gain their panoramic view. He detected puzzlement from them, as they soared high above him in the azure and nearly cloudless noontime sky. Their thoughts were not complex, but he detected a degree of confusion in their simple minds. He didn't sense fear in them, but they were wary of something that seemed unusual to them. This only added to the mystery and his excitement. "I'm really having an adventure," he thought to himself.

He stopped again and listened carefully, cupping his long ears forward and moving them from side to side sweeping the area in front of him. He heard nothing unusual, just the noises of the forest animals. He extended his mind again, this time to the forest animals and he again sensed the same confusion in them as the sea birds. He moved forward slowly now, gently picking his way through the dense underbrush toward what seemed to be a natural break in the limbs. He moved as quietly as possible given his size, using his upper arms to deflect brush from his sensing eye and his two lower visual eyes, all the while trying to keep his ears flattened against his head to avoid injury.

It was as he dodged the last snapping branch, almost stumbling out of the forest, that he simultaneously saw and sensed the minds of the strange creatures. He was startled that he had not sensed them before, but maybe it was because their thought patterns were so different. They just didn't register in his mind until it was too late. It was like suddenly becoming aware of a conversation in a crowded room, noisy with many people's thoughts. He chided himself, "How could I be so stupid and clumsy?"

He froze and concentrated on remaining as still as possible. He thought about running back into the forest cover, but he was surprised to find that he didn't feel a sense of panic. He was relieved that he didn't feel the need to run away because he wasn't sure his legs would move at that moment.

And just as quickly, they saw him. They began signaling to the ones who hadn't seen him and pointing in his direction. All of them stopped what they were doing and just looked at him. They were gathered around what must be the object that he had seen earlier that morning. He wondered if the object was a flying machine. The creatures remained as still as he did, neither party daring to even breathe. Tenge sensed surprise in them, like someone who is caught doing something secretive. And he sensed tension in them as well, but they made no moves toward Tenge or toward what seemed to be weapons on their belts. He was again surprised that he didn't feel afraid of these creatures. And then he realized that what he felt was the same tingling excitement he had been feeling since this adventure began. As Tenge searched with his mind, he thought he also saw intense curiosity in the beings.

They were about one third smaller than Tenge and had visible hair only on their round heads. They had two arms with hands as he did, as well as two legs. They apparently did not speak with their minds, because he heard them call softly to each other as did the Village children. They had two eyes, but apparently no third seeing-eye. They wore more clothes than he did and they had many tools and strange devices spread out on the grass around their sky-boat.

He wished that he had not crashed into the open meadow. He would have preferred to study these creatures before making himself known to them. Now it was too late to be coy. His mind raced. "I might be able to out run them. But there are a lot of them and they must be powerful if they can fly. They could probably come after me in their machine and catch me."

He reasoned that his best option was to do nothing and let them make the next move. This was, after all, the adventure he had come to explore. "Be in the moment, Tenge," he thought, trying to encourage himself. "And in the future be careful what you wish for."

CHAPTER 10

All men would be tyrants if they were able.
DANIEL DEFOE

Beta Continent

The life giving flow of neural energy coursing through her feeding tongue was invigorating for !Kerrt and bordered on the sensual. As she extended her mind she read a similar reaction from the male who was engorging himself not five meters from her. *You remain as wary of me as I am of you,* she thought to him. *A match made in hell,* she sneered between the gulps of tingling energy sliding over her tongue. *To save ourselves we have come to this?*

Ah, a rhetorical question from the hell bitch? !Zsakk countered with as much malice as he could project.

Be careful male. I could kill you easily from this distance!

And what do you think you would gain, you ingrate? Where's the thank you for saving your sorry ass... and mine? Besides, with our closeness and with our thoughts so intermingled, if you attack me it would probably kill you as well.

She thought about this and concluded he was probably right. *I'm just disgusted with myself for the compromising position I'm in. It's very hard not to feel sick just being here with a...male.*

He felt the revulsion in her thoughts, but also understood that much of her thoughts were just bravado. And he could feel her thankfulness for life, even though she would never voice it for fear of showing weakness. *Actually you can leave any time you want. I know you'd feel better—how did you say it?—by putting some distance between yourself and **the male**, as you choose to call me. My name is !Zsakk, female. So do me the honor of calling me by my name or get lost and fend for yourself.*

Her answer was apparent from her body language, as !Kerrt returned to her feeding and her threatening thoughts ebbed rapidly from their common consciousness.

They had managed to corner the herd and bring down two juveniles. The Ela had fought bravely defending their herd family, but the coordinated attack and paralyzing energy bolts were too much for the herd. It was no matter that the other Ela had escaped for the time being. Absorption of the life-giving neural energy required some time. And neither of the hunters wanted to waste any of the precious energy through haste.

She smirked at !Zsakk's brief tribute to their fallen prey. This was certainly a new twist for her. *For God's sake !Zsakk. I don't know how Others do it across the mountains, but we don't say grace over food here in this jungle. And besides, these are Ela. They are not like us. They're animals.*

After dragging their prey away from the retreating herd, !Kirrt didn't wait an instant before she savagely thrust her feeding tongue into the soft neck of the paralyzed, but living, juvenile Ela. She sensed the terror in her victim trapped beneath her massive paws. She luxuriated in the surges of adrenaline from the dying creature and the resulting neural discharges that increased to a frantic pitch. She looked up only long enough to see !Zsakk devouring his prey's essence and mind. She thought to him: *You're really no different than me, male. I see how philosophical you are when you're starving.*

But she was surprised to read in !Zsakk's mind a transient notion of pity for the Ela, beyond his seemingly empty tribute. But there was more. She could see his disgust for her. *You have a callous disregard for these noble creatures that sustain us, !Kerrt. This is wrong and you should wise up.*

Maybe I'll try to be more philosophical when I'm not starving... !Zsakk, she replied with a smirk.

The hunters had only suffered minor injuries from the powerful tails and hind feet of the Ela. These would mend quickly with the energy of a "full belly." As !Kerrt drank the neural energy of her prey, she sensed the thoughts of the Ela as its energy flowed through her nervous system and into her energy banks. She had never thought much about these flashing thoughts and perceptions of her victim. She wondered why she was now paying attention to these impressions as they flashed by her in kaleidoscopic fashion. By absorbing the juvenile Ela she experienced its life through its accumulated memories and thoughts. Mostly the thoughts consisted of herd life. But there was something more that she could not quite resolve. She saw the memory of the two hunters springing from the jungle and firing bolt after blinding bolt of energy at the panicked herd. This vision was especially vivid, probably because it was so new and so charged with emotion. It was panic in the minds of the herd, as well as the pain of the paralyzing bolts and the terror of impending death in their captives that increased the flow of the life giving energy that she so craved.

Interestingly, the Ela had been surprised to have been attacked by two hunters at once. !Kerrt saw no knowledge of this in the herd's collective memory. This confirmed for !Kerrt the uniqueness of their coordinated attack and her unusual relationship with !Zsakk. But there seemed to be something more in the thoughts of the life that flowed out of her kill and into her. The thoughts were illusive and floated just beyond her reach, like trying to recall a dream on awakening. The more she tried to grasp the thoughts the more they disintegrated like gossamer. She had never sensed these ill-defined notions before; none the less, they seemed strangely important now. "Maybe this Ela is special?" she wondered to herself. "Perhaps I'm just more focused because of my hunger. Maybe I'm just trying to glean every morsel I can and therefore I'm just more aware of their thoughts." She certainly couldn't remember being this close to the edge before. She realized with a shudder that she wouldn't have survived if the hunt had not been successful. She saw the same level of need and desperation in !Zsakk as she watched him voraciously devour his Ela with a greed that dispelled his eulogizing banter. Seeing his savagery forced her to think about their feeding orgy. "I guess we're both driven by the pheromones of blood lust that seem so thick in the air that I believe I could cut them with a claw. Maybe we're the animals, the savages, and not the Ela," she thought with a shudder.

And though she hated to admit it, !Zsakk had been right; neither of them would have survived without cooperation. As she warily observed him she felt a strange bond growing between them. "This is very odd," she thought. "What am I feeling for this…male?"

And why had she never considered cooperation with her kind before? The logic of collective security and cooperation had always been there in the thoughts of the Ela, and yet she had missed it over and over again. Why did it take a starving male to make her see the logic of cooperation? Was it hunger or something else that had made her see things differently? And now, where should the two of them go with this partnership that was indeed so…strange?

Her thoughts were interrupted by a warning from !Zsakk. *Be careful what you think !Kerrt. You eat so loudly and sloppily that your thoughts spill out to me. I can see in your mind your revulsion for me and Others of our kind.*

She responded: *Then you also are able to see all of my thoughts, not just the superficial emotions at the surface of my mind. Look deeper !Zsakk and don't try to manipulate me. Yes, the drool from your lips is disgusting. But something happened here that is important. You say you've never cooperated in a hunt before. So how did this idea come to you?*

He stopped his feeding and focused his mind on her: *I told you that cooperation suddenly seemed to be the only solution. The thought just came to me as we were both approaching the herd and I considered the prospects of fighting you, and then attacking them. I just knew that without cooperation both of us would fail and that we would die.*

She thought about his explanation and she didn't think he could deceive her even if that was his desire. *So what do you propose after we finish feeding? Usually, when our kind come this close, a mating is a negotiated result. I want to warn you, don't even think about it! The obvious reason is that the food supply is far too tenuous to sustain me through a pregnancy.*

Whoa, take it easy, !Kerrt; I'm not interested in sex! Actually, I haven't thought any further ahead than this meal and surviving the encounter with you. I really don't know what all this means or whether it means anything.

Well !Zsakk I think something happened here today that is unique for our kind. I think we should stay in this general area, hunt and explore this new relationship. My mind now seems flooded with fresh possibilities. Neither of us knows why we suddenly saw fit to cooperate and we should find out why we overcame our natural revulsion and chose to cooperate.

Fine, the male telepathed, as he turned away from her and back to the quivering Ela impaled on his feeding tongue. *But I'm not doing anything else till I finish my meal.*

It was easy to see the relish of his reply. It was tough to hide her revulsion in his feeding frenzy and with herself: *Disgusting aren't we?* she thought to no one in particular.

CHAPTER 11

Religion without science is blind and science without religion is
lame.
ALBERT EINSTEIN

The decision to send a landing party to both landmasses simultaneously was a first for Havel. It would make the operation more complex and more risky, but he thought it would be worth it. He admitted, at least to himself, that his decision was a bit self-serving since he would now lead one of the teams to make land-fall on G38-2. Hinton would lead the second team.

He and his executive officer had discussed the risks of both of them leaving the ship, but they quickly decided that their third in command, Lt. John Woolsey, was a capable officer and perfectly able to manage the ship in orbit. Besides, they were both itching to land and explore! And this would, of course, maximize the survey efficiency, they rationalized, while smiling and winking at each other.

The Alpha landmass was the most promising, since the long-range scans suggested constructions amid the vegetation. Havel took a captain's prerogative and decided that his team would land on the Alpha continent. He would take the ship's only linguist, Dr. Bill Walker and the xenobiologist, Linda Wade, with him. His boat would be flown by the back-up pilot and navigation officer, Barbara Grubb.

Commander Hinton would take the ship's Chief Geologist Bert Nixon with his team to the Beta continent in the southern hemisphere. From space the mountain ranges there seemed younger and more geologically active than those on the Alpha continent. It was felt that much of the discordant readings on their long-range scans were related to the somewhat unusual seismic activity on Beta and direct observations from the surface would be needed to clarify the mystery. Hinton also selected Chief Zoologist Jennifer Snyder for his team and Ensign Wise as his pilot. Both teams would carry a standard complement of three marines, as regulation mandated with any planetary landing. Sgt. Major Tom Cooper of the Space Marines would be in command of his two marines on the Beta boat. Sgt. Raymond Parrott would be in charge of his two marines on the Alpha boat.

Coordination of the landings and exploration would be through the ship under the direction of Lieutenant Woolsey, since direct communication between the two landing teams on different hemispheres would be limited and difficult. They stationed *Odyssey* in a geosynchronous orbit over Alpha in the northern hemisphere and deployed a communication satellite in a geosynchronous orbit over Beta. This allowed communications to be relayed between the landing teams and the ship. Havel and Hinton would be in control of their respective teams on the ground, while Mr. Woolsey would be in command of the ship and support the away teams. Fourteen of the ship's precious complement would be on the missions and any loss would strain the resources of the ship. "But the ship is designed with built-in redundancy of personnel and overlapping job training," Havel thought to himself for the hundredth time. "I know *Odyssey* can fly without me. So what if I'm exercising a little self interest to get down to the planet?" He had put this question to Hinton, Woolsey, and the senior staff and the opinion was that *Odyssey*'s operations would not be overtly compromised with the absent personnel. Even with the unthinkable loss of one or both landing crafts, *Odyssey* could limp home. The consensus was it was a calculated, but reasonable risk.

Yet the doubts of command flashed through Havel's mind as his boat and Hinton's left the *Odyssey* and began the breaking maneuvers for planet-fall. He told himself again and again the plan was sound, his people were good, their preparations were appropriate and this was the moment they had trained for all their adult lives. "Let it go, Jim; you've done all you can. The ship will be fine whether you are there to keep your eye on things or not. Trust in your training. Accept the risks and move on!" he muttered to himself through the clenched teeth of concern.

The thirty second burn of the boat's main engine interrupted the gut twisting effects of free fall and pushed them back into their padded seats. The engines shut down, after bleeding their orbital velocity, and weightlessness returned to Havel's temporary discomfort. His mind was soon distracted by the roar from the upper atmosphere of the planet as it began to howl against the hull plates of the stubby landing craft. Havel took a deep sigh and uttered a silent prayer. "Lord, keep us in the palm of your hand." He turned his attention to the instrument panel and began calling out velocity and altitude to Grubb in the pilot seat of the cockpit. "Focus on the job, Jim," he said to himself. "Be in the moment." They were going down to a planet that no human had ever seen. And there was the added possibility that there might be advanced life there to greet them. As a last check he looked over his shoulder to see that the crew and gear were secured and then returned to his job as co-pilot. He soon became lost in his job, as he scanned the instrument data stream and watched Pilot Grubb follow the glide path that the navigational computer had selected. The heads-up display on the forward window became Havel's whole world during the wild bouncing ride to the surface of a new world.

CHAPTER 12

You have to wonder about humans. They think Elvis is alive and
God is dead.
ANONYMOUS

Quixt continued his observation of the Terrans as he traveled to the
planet aboard the landing craft commanded by Captain Havel. It was
a simple matter for him to remain undetected among the Terrans. The
Quixt had long ago evolved to exist in other dimensional states. It
required minimal effort on his part to shift himself to a four dimensional
configuration and thus remain cloaked to the three dimensional Terrans.
It was as if he were sharing three dimensions of reality with them and
at the same time occupying an additional physical plane of reality.
He could be right there among them, continue his observation and
remain hidden while in this advanced special configuration. This same
ability allowed the *Quixt* to travel inter-dimensionally to any place in
the universe or to any of the other ten dimensions in existence since
the Creation. They even had the ability to move to other alternative
universes, but Quixt had never been asked to do so. He speculated
that because his species had evolved in a three dimensional universe,
the Progenitor kept them at work in the here and now. Often he
wondered what these other universes might be like and had thought
about exploring these possibilities, but pragmatism had always reigned.
"This is just useless speculation, Quixt," he told himself. "Best to
remain practical, Mr. Quixt and 'keep one's feet on the ground,' as
the Terrans...err humans would say. Pay attention to the problem at

hand. You've got plenty to do right here without getting abstract and theoretical," he chided himself.

Quixt evaluated the Terran's plans for exploring the G38-2, as they called Tenge's World. Considering their achievement of interstellar travel, it was remarkable how little preparation the Terrans had given the issue of first contact with another sentient species. They had safeguards in place to protect their home world should they encounter a more advanced and perhaps hostile species. There had been some training of the crew, but Quixt was amazed to find so little planning had been devoted to what contact would do philosophically to the Terran psyche and culture. He thought, "Perhaps their leaders don't really believe there are other thoughtful beings in the universe. The Terran Captain certainly believes that there must be other thoughtful life somewhere in the universe," but the ship's computer banks told Quixt humans had not yet encountered any advanced life form. He was equally amazed that the majority of Terrans didn't even consider other life, despite sending ships to the stars. Quixt thought, "What hubris humans possess to think they are alone and supreme! Well, they're in for a shock."

As the human landing craft crossed the terminator and descended toward a landing site, Quixt continued to weigh the options and said a prayer. *Lord, help me to be sensitive to your directives and help me do the right thing. The People certainly need a proverbial kick in the butt. The Others need help too, since they certainly don't use their skills effectively and may eventually starve without a sense of community that I've been trying to help them achieve. And the Terrans are about to get a big dose of "humble pie" as they call it. May I be up to the task of guiding all of them. It's going to get interesting!*

CHAPTER 13

The Creator...churns out the intricate texture of...the world
with a spendthrift genius and an extravagance of care.
ANNIE DILLARD

Alpha Continent

The Alpha team purposely set their landing craft down approximately
twenty kilometers from what appeared to be a village they observed on
their approach. Havel could barely keep himself composed let alone
direct his team. Everyone was at a window or looking at the heads-
up visual displays as the village passed in the distance. Walker almost
came out of his seat craning his neck to get a view of what had to be
the work of intelligent beings.

"Did you see that, Captain?" He continued without pause, his
voice about an octave higher than normal for him. "I wonder why we
couldn't make out the village from *Odyssey*. Captain, we're not alone
out here!"

"I saw it on the heads-up display, Bill. We recorded the fly-by
and when we sit down we can study it further. Please, everyone sit
down until we get the boat on the ground. I'm not your mother, but
there will be a time-out for anyone not strapped in. Barbara, we're at
four hundred meters and one hundred and ninety knots."

"Roger, Captain. The meadow ahead and to the starboard looks
like a good spot to land. I'll fly over it once to scan the underlying
strata, but it should be reasonable for a landing. These boats are tough

and are powerful enough to get us out even if we sink a bit into soft ground."

The actual touch-down, using the Harrier Jump Jet-like vertical thrusters, was actually anticlimactic, considering the excitement of the approach. Havel was glad when Grubb cycled down the screaming vertical thrusters and he felt the welcome bump and lurch as the stubby landing struts touched down and settled ever so slightly into the foreign soil.

Pvt. Stephanie Foulk exclaimed, "We made it!" capturing everyone's sentiment.

Jeff Venable, the other marine private turned and gave her a high five, breaking the tension. He shouted, "Way to go, Ensign Grubb!" congratulating her on getting them down safely. Grubb barely acknowledged him with a "humph" as she and Havel were already going through the post flight check list.

Executing the mission plan, Linda Wade quickly turned to the starboard hull instruments and activated the bio-analyzer that emitted a soft whirring as it began to scan the outside air for obvious pathogens. They all crowded around to watch the numbers spin rapid-fire like a slot machine. No one dared breathe till the indicator read zeros all the way across. After looking at her watch, Wade saw that the whole process had occurred in less than three minutes; she would have guessed an hour! Sgt. Raymond Parrott then stepped back from looking over her shoulder and moved to aft the hatch. He placed his hands on the auto cycling air lock mechanism and then looked at the Captain. Havel nodded and the Sergeant broke the hatch and they all felt their ears pop as they adjusted to the different atmospheric pressure. The morning sun streamed through the hatch and with it came a flood of moist air. Sergeant Parrott extended the debarkation ramp and then he and his marines exited first, weapons ready. Havel next stepped to the hatch's edge and gazed out on a new world! He suddenly thought of Neil Armstrong, the Apollo astronaut who first stepped onto the moon. Havel had stepped onto foreign worlds before, but this one just felt different in an unidentifiable way. The air was warm and felt more humid than the dry and sterile air of the ship. It reminded him of getting out of a plane in Florida on a balmy spring day. He felt a gentle breeze on his cheek and he inhaled *real* fresh air, rather than the ship's recycled and filtered air that somehow always smelled sterile. "But there was something else," he thought; "something alien and exciting, and smells... exotic—like the curry and ginger that I smelled in the spice market of Istanbul with Becky years ago! Perhaps it's a bit more humid than I'd like, but overall quite nice," he thought to himself. "It's especially nice after being cooped up in the ship for the last two and a half months." He could even smell the unmistakable scent of the sea on the inland breeze.

They walked down the ramp together to stand in a place that no man had ever stood. They were on a grassy meadow that had a rolling slope surrounded by a forest about sixty meters away. Havel immediately noted the deepened color of the vegetation and the azure sky. It was like seeing colors through a Polaroid filter that reduced reflected light and led to a greater depth of colors. He thought that the sky was a bit bluer than Earth's. It was like the sky that you see from higher elevations in the mountains. And the wispy clouds had a bit of a pink tint to them, like those seen in a late afternoon sunset.

Havel shook himself from personal impressions and ordered the marines to secure the perimeter and set up the defensive energy screen. He especially enjoyed the scientists as they gleefully studied everything. Havel decided not to bother them with housekeeping chores, but to let them explore around the boat to their hearts' desire. He did order everyone to stay within thirty meters of the boat until everything was secure and until he gave further orders.

Their data suggested that the air and their immediate environment were safe; at least as safe as one could expect of an alien planet. They detected no electromagnetic transmissions, either during their descent or now at the landing site. Their initial scans and impressions were reviewed by *Odyssey*, but despite Alpha's data and a more focused investigation of the "village" from orbit, nothing showed up conclusively. Everyone was wondering whether the village could be an illusion or some ancient structure long since abandoned.

They had timed their landing to occur just after dawn to give them a full day of exploration before returning to the ship by nightfall. It was possible to stay on the planet overnight if necessary, but the quarters in the boat would be quite cramped and Havel wasn't sure they would be secure enough to safely stay on the planet after dark, despite the energy screen.

Havel recognized that his sense of smell was less acute than most and especially not as acute as many women's. He wondered what Dr. Wade and Private Foulk, the two women, thought of the exotic smells. He liked the strange fragrances given off by the colorful flowering plants in the meadow around them. And the trees of the forest a short distance away also sported numerous colorful flowering appendages that were perhaps adding to the smells.

"It's just so beautiful!" he thought. He knew he should be focusing on details of the landing; he was just thankful that Sergeant Parrott and his marines were apparently not as distracted by the beauty and newness around them and went about their business.

They already knew that the air would be breathable; spectrometric studies from orbit told them the oxygen, nitrogen and the concentrations of the other minor atmospheric components. But the feel and smells of an alien world were beyond a scientific analysis. "To be outdoors in coveralls, out of the confines of a carbon steel hull was exhilarating!" Havel thought.

It didn't take long for them to break a sweat in the warm sunlight as they worked to set up their base camp. Havel especially enjoyed watching the youthful exuberance of his biologist, Linda Wade, as she ran about with her data recorder and specimen pouch. "She's in a xenobiologist's heaven," Havel thought. "And perhaps this is a place like heaven; this world is beautiful!"

There was no warning when the alien came out of the forest. Pvt. Jeff Venable was the first to see the creature. He sent a chilling, "Captain, look!" through the com-link and pointed excitedly toward the forest. Havel flinched as a shiver of apprehension spread through him as the alarm sounded. He crouched slightly and pivoted to look in the direction Venable was pointing. He saw the alien not forty meters away! Havel had the immediate impression that he was looking at a mythological faun or satyr as depicted in allegorical art works that he had studied in college and had seen in art books. Here before them was the most advanced alien life form ever encountered by humans. Havel was stunned as emotions washed over him. Here was complex life among the stars as he had always imagined must exist somewhere.

Havel sensed that the alien creature was equally shocked to come upon them. It was about one third larger than a human and had a large triangular head. Especially compelling were the three eyes that aesthetically echoed the triangular head. Havel thought it was quite remarkable that the alien's gaze met theirs evenly and without apparent fear. Havel thought to himself, "This big fellow must be one cool customer to come on something so strange as seven humans and a spacecraft and still stand his ground." Havel wondered if the reaction to them was an animal's naive response or a measured reaction due to intelligence. "I don't think I'd be so calm if the circumstances were reversed," Havel admitted to himself.

The alien stood on two powerful hind legs and had two upper arms capped by easily identifiable hands that were "thankfully empty," Havel thought. The creature was partially clothed in a simple rust colored garment. The alien seemed to be covered with short brindle colored hair everywhere except for the large head that had a receding hairline and longer hair that flowed down almost to its shoulders like a mane. The hair seemed to have an iridescent sheen, like a drop of oil floating on the surface of water. There were also what appeared to be two large ears that seemed to angle toward them as if to increase acuity. And to further support the notion of intelligence, there was a small pouch slung over the shoulders. Havel saw no sign of a weapon.

Havel looked around at his crew and saw that none of them had moved. "Everyone, keep still," Havel whispered through the com-link. "This is the moment we've trained for all of our lives and the reason we've come fifty light-years. Ms. Grubb, I don't want you to leave the boat and I want you to slowly lock the laser canon on the… 'faun.' But you are not to fire unless I order you to do so. Do you understand, Barbara?"

"Yes, Captain," came the tense response of the pilot from the landing craft.

Havel continued as calmly and as softly as he could, given the tenseness of the situation. "Dr. Wade, I want you and Dr. Walker to slowly walk to my position. No weapons, people! We came here in peace and I want the mission to stay on this footing."

As his xenobiologist and linguist made their way slowly forward, Havel observed that the creature remained still and did not retreat into the relative safety of the forest. Havel actually sensed that the creature was interested in them and even curious; "It's not afraid," Havel thought to himself. "I would be if I were alone and came upon a bunch of aliens."

"Bill, do you get any impressions from the alien?" whispered Havel.

"Yeah, Captain. I think I do!" came the hushed but excited reply. "I can't put my finger on it, but there's something there beyond just the body language. I know this sounds illogical, but I believe it's trying to communicate with us. I don't know how to explain this sensation, Captain. Is anyone else sensing anything from the alien? What about you, Linda?"

"I agree with you, Bill. I don't understand it; and what I'm sensing is a bit creepy," Wade whispered through the com-link.

Then everyone else chimed in at once reporting the same sensations, all beginning shortly after the alien appeared in the meadow.

"It feels as though I'm seeing things from the alien's perspective," Walker whispered.

"Pilot, please verify that these pictures and our impressions are being received by the ship," said Havel.

"We are recording and transmitting real-time, Captain," responded Grubb with a bit less than her usual dryness.

"OK, Bill, you and I are going to slowly take off our tool belts and weapons and then we're going to walk very slowly toward the alien with our hands open and empty. I want you to put your recording translator in your pocket. I don't want to lose any vocalizations from the alien or the opportunity to collect data that might help us to construct a language base. Understand?"

"Yeah," came the quiet and terse response from the usually talkative linguist.

"Linda, I want you to stay here. I don't want too many of us crowding him."

Havel was thankful that Wade's simple "OK" belied no irritation. They removed their belts and then moved about fifteen meters closer to the alien. Havel detected no change in its demeanor. As they got closer to the alien, Havel was again drawn to the creature's eyes. The two lower ones were a bright and piercing yellow with a large blackened center; probably a pupil he thought. It was the upper eye that was more captivating. This apical eye had a pale bluish hue, but was otherwise opalescent and without a pupil. It did not move or seem to make eye contact as the lower yellow eyes did. Havel imagined that the eye could *see* right through him, despite the illogic of such a thought.

As they stood there facing the alien Havel suddenly decided on an impulse to voice a simple "Hello" with his right hand raised and open. He would later wonder why he hadn't prepared something more memorable. But in all his years of training and thinking about first contact it had just never occurred to him to think about what to say. He thought, "How odd that all of our training was focused on the process and not the moment."

The alien did not immediately react to Havel's overture. The creature met Havel's gaze with its two lower eyes and then ever so slightly cocked its head to the side. The gesture made Havel think of a similar turn of the head when his dog heard something unusual. The responding vocalization that came from the alien was musical and even pleasant and had a plaintive quality.

"Could you get anything from that, Bill?"

"No sir. We'll need a lot more vocalizations to begin to build a comparative vocabulary. None of us has any real experience with first contact, Sir. We have protocols for a beginning, but they've never been field tested for obvious reasons. Sir, I still feel so…unusually calm."

"I feel the same way, Bill," said Havel. "I know I should feel excited, yet I don't feel an adrenaline rush. Shouldn't we be feeling excited, Linda?"

"I don't know, Captain. Apparently, we all feel similarly. I know we've all been well trained, but I don't think this explains what we're feeling," observed the biologist.

Wade continued, "The real question is 'Why?' And it seems that our friend here is also extraordinarily calm under what should be an extreme situation for it as well. But then how can I logically say what is normal for him, or her, or it? We have no basis to conclude anything at this point other than that he is in control of himself, has responded to our overture and this speaks of intelligence. I think he feels he is an equal in this situation. How can that be, Sir? Maybe he has reinforcements in the forest. Perhaps we should take a more defensive posture."

"No, I don't think so," said Havel. "I don't believe we're in any danger and our scans were negative. We're going to continue with a cautious, but trusting, posture; after all we're on his world. Ensign Grubb, do you see any anything else in our area?"

"No, Sir. And I took the liberty of scanning the area actively. I'm sure he's alone, aside from a few very small animals in the area."

"Thank you, Barb. Dr. Walker, would you have just walked out of the forest to check out a strange group of aliens that you encountered?"

"Hell no, uh...excuse me, Sir. I totally agree, Captain. I wouldn't have showed my hand unless I was in control of the situation. I don't see any evidence of technology in his possession that might give him an edge."

"I don't either," Wade interjected from a short distance behind them. She went on, "Perhaps we're confronting an entity that knows it's in his element, and technology is not the trump card. Perhaps it's arrogance on our part to think we have the advantage because we think we have superior technology and there are more of us."

The alien continued to look at them, turning its head from side to side and directing its ears back and forth following the conversation of the humans. "Is it a weakness to feel so secure?" Havel wondered.

"People, I believe the order of the day is carpe diem," said Havel. "This is our moment. I'm going to move forward and meet our 'neighbor.' Sergeant Parrott!"

"Yes, Sir!"

"You will assume command of the away-team if anything happens to me. In that event your primary mission is to get the team back to the ship and you are not to attempt any rescue efforts that might jeopardize the crew or the overall mission. Is that clear, Ray?"

"Yes, Captain. But... are you sure this is a wise move, Sir?"

"I'll let you know in a few minutes, Sergeant," said Havel, trying to keep fear out of his voice as he moved forward to meet their visitor.

CHAPTER 14

A job is the way to make a living; Service is the way to make a life.
ARTHUR ASHE

Beta Continent

The vastness of the ocean in the forward view screen was what struck Steve Hinton as they descended toward the blue-green planet. Their reentry vector had carried them around the planet, bleeding off their orbital velocity. Now on the tactical heads-up display he could see the Beta continent coming up over the horizon in the distance. The approaching land mass gave a hint of green and brown color, but everything else was blue ocean and blue sky.

They continued their scanning all during the descent to the southern continent, but again failed to detect any organized structures, confirming the pre-flight impressions. All the view-ports were taken by crewmembers as they craned their necks to see below. As spectacular as the view might be, Hinton remained busy on the flight deck assisting Ensign Wise guide the boat to a landing site.

Hinton noted the lack of the usual chatter from the marines and smiled to himself. Apparently the view of this new world was entertaining enough. Perhaps they were thinking of how special it was to fly over an alien ocean and land on a world never seen by humans. They approached the coastal mountain range and flew low over the forested foothills running along the coast that seemed to stretch to both horizons. Hinton thought to himself, "An empty world and a beautiful one."

"Commander, I believe we'll be able to get good seismic readings from the foothills below the costal ridge."

"Thank you, Dr. Nixon," said Hinton. "Joanna, what do you think of that grassland area just above the beach dunes as a possible landing site? I believe it's close enough for us to access the forest relatively easily from that position."

"I see it, Sir," said Wise as she banked the boat to the port and took a quick glance out the side cockpit window. "It looks like a good site as long as the ground is not too sandy and soft. Of course, we won't know for sure till we set the boat down, but I want to be at least several hundred meters away from the shore line as a matter of safety. She's a tough craft; I can pull her out of anything short of quick sand."

Wise continued her slow turn simultaneously bleeding speed and altitude by extending the cowl flaps on the boat's stubby wings. Hinton heard and felt the station-keeping thrusters engage underneath the ship. The trick was to slowly engage these vertical thrusters as the ship's horizontal momentum was lost. A smooth transition would lead to a controlled landing. The concept was centuries old, but still required an accomplished pilot to make the transition.

Coming in over the southwestern coast, Hinton left the details of the landing to his pilot, focusing his attention on the ground rising towards them. Wise scouted the site by making several passes over the meadow while Hinton scanned the sub-terrain for rock. The actual touch down was gentle and Hinton felt the boat settle onto solid ground.

"*Odyssey*, Beta has landed," Wise radioed triumphantly back to the ship in orbit. Joanna's choice of words made Hinton smile as he recalled the first landing on the moon in the mid-twentieth century.

"Roger, Beta," came the quick and reassuring reply from the ship.

Hinton assisted Wise to quickly cycle through the instrument checklist verifying the boat's status. Sergeant Cooper reported that additional scans of their immediate vicinity were clear. Dr. Snyder operated the bio-filters which soon registered the all clear, just like the report from the Alpha team that had been relayed to Hinton during their final approach. Though the result was expected, Hinton realized this continent was half a world away and might have unique contagions. He hoped it would also have unique fauna and flora. He wasn't jealous of the Captain on Alpha; he was just excited by the prospects of his own team's discoveries.

Exiting the boat amid the beauty of the empty meadow with its yellow and green grass-like foliage and breathing the air of a foreign world was simply "wondrous," sighed Hinton. He was struck by the superficial similarity to an Earth meadow rising above coastal sand dunes. He toyed with the idea of not posting marine sentries, but regulations governing landing protocols demanded he do so. He remembered his old tactical professor, Maj. Pat Marret, at the Academy. Her words rang in his ears even now as he deployed his team. "You've got to pay attention to details," the old gal preached. "The security of your personnel and the success of your mission are as dependent upon good planning as they are on execution!" He remembered rolling his eyes at the "old pedagogue," as they called her. "But how right she was; it was just my youth that made me not appreciate her wisdom at the time," he reflected.

As they readied themselves for exploration, Hinton could barely restrain Snyder from running off to study literally everything. She nearly ran into the side of the boat while gazing through her binoculars, marveling at what she thought "must be sea birds out over the ocean". Hinton couldn't really blame Snyder. How could you not be fascinated and curious about the obviously sophisticated flying creatures circling high above them in the distance? The pink tinge to the cumulous clouds high in the azure sky and the strange sweet smells of the flowering plants of the grassland only added to the wonder and the mystery of the moment.

"This is what I was made for!" Hinton suddenly realized. All the long years of education and training had been full of challenges, but challenges that he overcame. And now, everything he had worked for had come together in his career and this landing. "But this is more than anything I could have imagined," he thought to himself. He examined his feelings and thought about how he felt the first time he walked to the south rim of the Grand Canyon. He was awestruck then and now this experience was even more wondrous. He was not a philosophical man like the Captain, but he allowed himself a brief moment of reflection. "Maybe the Captain is right in one respect. Maybe there *is* more than just what we see and can prove." Hinton smiled at his analytic nature as he found himself critiquing his feelings of the moment. "How odd," he thought to himself, "that this place is special to me in a way I didn't think was possible. Is this what they refer to as an epiphany, a new understanding of things?" he wondered. "For the first time I can appreciate something beautiful that transcends the knowledge of photons simply striking my retina and activating neural-chemical impulses." He remembered the Captain droning on several weeks ago about the difference between "the Classic and the Romantic Period." Havel had used the example of light that produces sight. The romantics proclaimed beauty and the sublime while empiricists wrote equations to explain how things worked. "And now I understand for the first time; this place makes me appreciate beauty and wonder as never before."

"Sorry to break into your thoughts, Commander, but I'd like to leave our body armor here," said Sergeant Cooper. "Our scans for hostiles have been negative and it's pretty warm to take a hike in that gear."

"Its okay, Sergeant Major; I need to get back and focus on our job. It's just so damn beautiful after being cooped up in the ship for months."

"Yes Sir, it is beautiful," responded the Sergeant, who was all marine and all business.

Hinton wondered to himself whether the sergeant had even looked at the world around him. "Well, it's time to get back to the business of organizing this crew," he told himself. "Stay sharp, Hinton! There'll be plenty of time for reflection later."

Returning to his command persona, Hinton reviewed the plan that he and Havel had worked out on *Odyssey*. "Guys and Gals, circle up; here's the plan. I'm going to take a scouting party up to the forest," as he pointed over his left shoulder, "and then we'll circle back toward the landing site along the shoreline about two kilometers north of the boat's position. We'll take provisions for the day and I want Dr. Snyder to go with me as well as Sergeant Cooper and Private Grieve. Jenny and I will carry our laser side arms, but Sergeant, I want you and Grieve to carry your plasma rifles. I anticipate being away for about six hours and this should give Dr. Nixon plenty of time to do his seismic survey work. We'll make a decision about spending the night on the planet this evening. Corporal Green and Ensign Wise, you'll stay with the boat and assist Dr. Nixon. Any questions?"

"No Sir," snapped the marines.

"Sir, I'll track you with the GPS," said Green. "Of course we'll be in radio contact, and may I recommend touching base with each other hourly?"

"Good suggestion, Corporal. I can see why Sergeant Cooper speaks so highly of you," responded Hinton.

"Thank you, Sir."

"Corporal, calibrate the GPS system to track the signal in each of our watches." And speaking loudly enough that even the distracted scientists could hear him, "Everyone is to keep their communicators and sidearms with them at all times." While not singling out the scientists, Hinton emphasized, "I don't want anyone to be so distracted by their work that they lose their equipment."

Nixon and Snyder managed to look up from their observations long enough to acknowledge the overall plan, but they were far too distracted to worry much about logistical questions other than which instruments they needed. Hinton noted that Nixon quickly checked to see that his sidearm was on his tool belt.

"Dr. Snyder, where is your sidearm?" asked Hinton as they left the landing site.

As she fumbled with her equipment belt it was obvious that her weapon was not there. They all waited as she hurried back to retrieve her weapon. "I'm sorry Commander, but I've only shot the thing once or twice so it's not a big part of my life."

"I understand, Jenny, but something bad might try to bite you and then you'd wish you had the weapon," kidded Hinton.

"Well, I just figured that Sergeant Cooper or Private Grieve would save little ole me," Snyder replied in her best fake southern drawl while batting her eyes in a mocking fashion.

With Cooper on point, the survey party worked their way up the gentle slope through the thigh high vegetation that they all agreed was very similar to the wispy grasses of Earth's Great Plains. Snyder was simply ecstatic over everything and would have been happy to just sit down in the field under the early morning sun and categorize the grasses and the small insect-like creatures that the group flushed as they walked.

"These look like grasshoppers!" she shouted with excitement. "Did you see that one? I've seen at least three different types of these things, though they all seem to have the same basic pattern." Holding a specimen about two centimeters long between her fingers, she pointed to the row of three structures across its forehead. "These must be the equivalent of eyes. I wonder what electromagnetic spectrum they visualize."

Grieve said, "Doc, you ought not to pick up that bug with your bare hands. That varmint might sting you or be poisonous."

Hinton responded with as little exasperation in his voice as he could muster. "Jenny, I can appreciate your passion about everything, but I want to get to the other side of the forest by noon. I'm sure you'd be content to cordon off a three by three meter section of grassland next to the boat and count every bug and blade of grass there. But let's stay focused on our mission today; we're here to do a superficial survey and gain an overall perspective of this area. We're not here to do basic science; that will come later. And Grieve is right. I don't want you to pick up anything with your bare hands and put yourself at risk until we know more about this world and its creatures."

"Yeah, I know, I know," she said simultaneously holding up her hand to ward off the lecture and releasing her specimen. "It's just so damn exciting! There's so much to see. Look at the size of that *bug*!" She had stopped again and was pointing to something crawling along the stalk of a bush. "That one's a good eight centimeters long. Look, it's got the same arrangement of structures on its triangular head. Those have to be eyes," she said out loud to herself and anyone else who would listen. "It's got three sets of legs and don't you think it looks a lot like a praying mantis?" she asked her group who just kept walking.

Looking back at the dawdling scientist, Cooper turned and walked back to Snyder's side. Cooper growled, "Take a picture, Doc, and move on!" Despite his gruffness, Hinton noted that Cooper gently grabbed the pretty scientist's arm and pulled her forward toward the forest.

Together the group found a way to entice Snyder forward by promising her larger and more exciting specimens in the forest. But as they walked they still had to endure her incessant pointing and descriptions that served to supplement her camera recordings.

Hinton was content to just be on this strange and beautiful world. The 1.1 earth-mass of the planet and the consequent greater gravity made their efforts a bit tougher, but otherwise the slope wasn't too bad. The artificial gravity field of the ship and the regular workout regimen had served to keep them all in fairly good physical condition. And the slightly higher 22% oxygen content of the atmosphere partially compensated for the greater exertion. Hinton knew that there was a bit more carbon dioxide and a mild reduction in nitrogen, but "all in all very breathable," he thought. In fact, he considered this world, and especially this uninhabited continent, to be ideal for colonization. And humans on Beta wouldn't interfere with the Alpha continent a half world away even if intelligent life were discovered there.

The sun felt warm on Hinton's back and he didn't mind the humidity that was higher than ship's standard. After being on the *Odyssey* for the last several months, he especially enjoyed the open sky that was a deeper blue than Earth's. As they stopped to catch their breath, Hinton looked back toward the boat that he could see about a kilometer away. He felt a light breeze on his face as it rose from the sea below and he could smell the sea on the wind.

"Do you smell that, Jenny? I smell the salt spray of the sea! Do you think there could be this much similarity in all Earth-like planets?"

"Well, it's certainly possible, Commander. We've never found another planet that is this similar to Earth. Others have studied the evolution of isolated ecosystems on Earth and then speculated on evolution elsewhere. There are always similarities to be found in even diverse systems, but of course these systems arose from a common source, our own Earth. The real speculation has always been whether we would find homology on an alien world with similar composition as Earth's."

"Homo-what?" grunted Cooper.

"Not 'homo,' Sergeant! I said homology; it means similarity. The question as to whether another world might develop similarly to Earth may finally be answered here. This would be the greatest discovery in the biological sciences in our time. You may be making history, Sergeant!" smiled the gleeful Snyder.

"Humph," was all she could get out of the crusty sergeant who incessantly scanned the underbrush and the approaching forest.

"Hey, Commander, I don't know as much as the Doc, but I do know it's great to stretch my legs at something more purposeful than the treadmill on the ship," shouted the young Grieve as they marched onward toward the forest now only a few hundred meters away.

Hinton glanced over the heads of his small column. He found that a position at the rear of their column was best to keep Snyder from wandering off to film a new "bug" and holding up their march.

"These grasses seem to be much like Earth's, Commander," continued Snyder thoughtfully. "The prairie grassland on Earth has amazing diversity. I've now counted about a dozen different species of these insect-like creatures that I could spend years studying."

Just as she was speaking a larger animal was flushed by Grieve. "Wow, did you see that?" shouted the excited Snyder, as she pointed to a clump of purple tinted bushes under which the creature had scurried. "It was about the size of a cat. And it had six legs and the same row of three eyes across its triangular forehead!"

"Yeah, I saw it, Doc," said Grieve lowering his plasma rifle. "It scared the shit out of me. I almost fried the little bastard."

"Very impressive, Jenny; I told you we'd find larger animals closer to the forest," smiled Hinton.

As they resumed their march Cooper became uncharacteristically philosophical. "It's like fishing, Doc; the smaller fish gather near the underwater cover of sunken trees and bushes. This affords them protection. Then bigger fish come to feed where the smaller fish congregate. We'll probably see bigger 'fish' in the forest. Now that's homology you can study."

"Excellent analogy, Sergeant, and a challenging hypothesis. If we find this to be true, I'll call this *Cooper's Homology of Comparative Planetary Evolution.* You see, you're a scientist after all! A scientist is really nothing but a careful observer of the world."

"Well, that's enough science for me, Ma'am. My job is to keep something big from taking a bite out of your booty, pardon my French."

"No offense taken, Tom. I'd like to keep all my parts with me," countered Snyder.

"Commander, I want to reiterate my concerns about the forest," said Cooper. "My helmet's heads-up tactical display will be limited in there. We'll need to take it real slow and be alert for hostiles," observed Cooper.

"Your concerns are noted, Sergeant Major. The Captain and I discussed this in mission planning. We'll proceed slowly but we will proceed," said Hinton with conviction.

At the forest's edge they stopped to rest again in the shade of *trees* that towered above them. Hinton noted that the larger ones stood perhaps fifty to sixty meters tall and their overall appearance was remarkably similar to aspen groves in the American West. The trunks all had a smooth surface and a blue-green color. The foliage was a blend of yellow and green with deep purple veins that spread out on what appeared to be leaves. The shade was welcome to Hinton who was sweating from the exertion of their climb. He could now hear the calls of animals that seemed to come from the forest treetops. There had only been the buzz of insects in the grassland. Hinton turned to see everyone looking up to try and spot one of the noisy creatures— everyone except Sergeant Cooper, who continued to survey the dense forest with suspicion and a furrowed brow. Looking back down the slope Hinton could see the blue-green ocean in the distance and the pink-tinged white clouds. "What a vision," he thought to himself. "How lucky I am to be here and experience such wonder."

Hinton noted the tension in Cooper's voice as he commented on the tactical aspects of entering the dense undergrowth. "Sir, I recommend we put our proximity radar in a continuously active mode when we move into the forest. This will augment our tactical vision a bit. Those calls we are hearing must be from larger animals and might pose some risk to us."

"I agree, Tom. Make it so." Hinton appreciated Cooper's caution. But Hinton did not want to come up short of the goals the

Captain and he had agreed upon in pre-mission planning. And he didn't want to fail on his first away- team assignment.

"Sergeant, you and Mr. Grieve take the point and Jenny and I will follow and cover your booties."

Cooper again managed a "humph" at the thought of "civvies" covering a marine's butt. He grabbed his private's arm and shoved him forward. "Come on, Grieve. This is why we get paid the big bucks," Cooper snarled. "You fan out on the left and I'll stay parallel to you on the right."

"Okay, Sarge." As he moved into the tree line, Grieve swept the forest ahead with his proximity radar. "All clear ahead to at least one hundred meters, I think."

"We can't be dependant on our instruments in this dense forest, Dave," said Cooper. "Stay sharp, and trust your instincts."

They checked in with the boat and their signal was good. Corporal Green informed them that there was nothing on the look-down satellite images and that Dr. Nixon was immersed in his work. "Let us know if our GPS signal weakens, Corporal."

"Aye, Sir!" came the simultaneous and reassuring voices of both Wise and Green.

As they entered the forest Hinton admitted to himself that "it's good to know they're looking over our shoulders."

It took a few minutes for their eyes to adjust to the relative darkness of the forest after the bright sun of the open grassland. The continuous forest canopy allowed only subdued light despite the mid-morning sun high overhead. The canopy was interlaced with vines that streamed downward to the forest floor. These vines were reddish and sported soft green and deep purple leaves that they soon discovered had very sharp edges. The blue-green bark of the trees contributed to the darkness of the forest, but "what an adventure!" Hinton reflected over and over in his mind.

The chatter of animals in the trees continued despite the noise the team made as they pushed and chopped through the underbrush. Snyder was the first to spot one of the animals in the treetops and excitedly tried to point out the creature high above them.

"Do you see it? Do you see it, guys? And do you see what it's doing? It's brachiating from branch to branch! There are several of them together up there. They're hard to see because their chartreuse coloring blends so well with the foliage. How many arms do you count?" Snyder asked the team.

"I see them, Doc!" exclaimed Grieve. "I count six arms and legs. Skittish little devils, aren't they? I think they look a lot like monkeys."

"They sure do, David," said Snyder. "I'd sure like to get a better look at them, but they're too high and are moving away now. I wish we had the time and the equipment to get up there and observe them closely."

"I'm glad we don't have to argue with you about climbing trees, Jenny," said Hinton. "I sort of like their screeching. It reminds me of the Howler Monkeys of the rain forests in Central America."

"Good observation, Steve. I agree with you." Snyder had her field glasses to her eyes trying to follow the creatures and was brought to her senses when she ran into the side of a tree.

"Careful, Doc," said Cooper as he helped her stand up and extricate herself from the vines. "I don't want to have to carry you out of this thicket."

After the retreat of the "monkeys" the forest grew very quiet as they trudged along in single file. Cooper's curiosity got the best of him and he had to ask, "What's brachiating Doc?"

Hinton noted that Snyder easily slipped into a teacher's style as she responded, "Brachiating is when monkeys swing from limb to limb using their arms. Perhaps this will be another chapter in your book Sergeant."

"Yeah, sure," growled Cooper.

Hinton decided to enter the discussion. "Jenny, have you noticed the absence of any bird-like creatures like we saw over the ocean? On Earth the forests have lots of birds that contribute to the noise of the forest."

"Hmm" Snyder mumbled quietly. "Steve, that's another interesting observation. You guys are great to explore with! But as for the noise of 'birds' that we saw over the ocean, we don't know whether they even vocalize as our birds do on Earth. There's just so much to explore and consider. You realize that your forced march, bypassing all these mysteries, is killing me."

"Yeah, I know I'm torturing you, Jenny," replied Hinton somewhat sarcastically. "Enjoy the moment and the whole experience for a change. There is more here than just analysis of the parts. Think about the whole, the big picture."

"Why you're beginning to sound like a Romantic era philosopher, Steve, just like the Captain!" exclaimed the scientist. "Maybe that's why you two get along so well."

"I doubt it, Jenny, but I have to admit that the Captain and the beauty of this world have made me think. And don't worry about the mysteries around us. There'll be plenty of time to study this world. *Odyssey* won't be leaving this planet anytime soon. This world is what we've come fifty light-years to find."

Conversation became increasingly difficult as they laboriously chopped their way through the underbrush, dodging the vines with the sharp leaves. Numerous small creatures with six legs went scurrying beneath the team's feet as they plodded on. Even Snyder was forced into silence as she had to concentrate on her footing. As best they could tell, all the creatures had the same three eyes arrayed in either a triangular or horizontal configuration across their foreheads. Grieve flushed one larger creature that had a reddish orange fur-like coat and emitted a faint mewing noise as it scurried from its hiding place in the underbrush.

About a half kilometer into the forest, the two marines came upon the most interesting discovery yet. They found wide swaths of forest pushed aside and trampled down. Snyder found lots of three toed foot prints and scat droppings that she thought indicated herbivores.

"Commander, these signs are from huge animals!"

Hinton smiled at the scientist. "Exciting isn't it?"

They decided to follow the trail since it was easier walking and it was in the general direction they were heading. And everyone wanted to catch a glimpse of the big animals; well, everyone except Sergeant Cooper, who seemed ever wary.

The simultaneous crack of energy and a blinding flash, in the relative darkness of the forest, was the only warning that they were under attack. Private Grieve instinctively crouched as he spun to look back toward the flash. He saw Commander Hinton collapsing to the forest floor and then he saw a great panther-like creature poised ten meters beyond in the underbrush. He momentarily froze as he saw the Commander falling and when he saw the alien. This proved fatal.

A second energy beam caught him squarely in the chest and knocked him backwards. He was vaguely aware of shouts and flashes around him, but he was falling—falling in slow motion as the world collapsed into darkness.

CHAPTER 15

As long as you love, you will see me in the stars.
CINDY BULLENS

Beta Continent

From a restless sleep born of an empty belly, !Kerrt was awakened at dawn by the thoughts of what could only be a new herd of Ela. It had been twenty three day-cycles since their last kill. This had really tested the new relationship between !Zsakk and her. The herd that they had first hunted together was gone. After relentless pursuit and repeated attacks, there were only a few stragglers left and these were scattered over thousands of hectares. Hunger had again become the only thing they could think about. And they were both increasingly edgy.

Wake up, male. I sense Ela!

You're not very pleasant when you're hungry, my dear, !Zsakk quipped as he awakened and stretched muscles still tired and sore from last night's long and fruitless hunt. As he turned to face her snarl and bared fangs he added: *And not in the mood for humor, I see.*

Expanding his own senses he too picked up the thoughts of the Ela. He turned his head gently from side to side as if trying to triangulate a distant sound. He telepathed: *The thoughts are a bit odd don't you think? Perhaps they're just a good distance away.*

She considered: *I don't think it's the distance, but I agree the thoughts are unusual. I actually think the herd is pretty close to us. Maybe it's a new defensive tactic of the Ela; after all, we've adapted, why can't they?*

97

But she really didn't think this was a realistic possibility. She considered the more likely reason to be their hunger and their desperation to avoid the privation of the past that nearly killed them both. Could that desperation cloud their judgment and perceptions?

!Zsakk seemed to be thinking the same thing when he thought: *We've got to be careful, !Kerrt, that our hunger doesn't cause us to make mistakes.*

Yes, I've considered that, she replied with a measure of exasperation if not resignation. *But what can we do about it? The solution is food. So what do you want to do, !Zsakk? These are the only Ela that we've come across in many day-cycles. We don't have a lot of choice, do we?*

!Zsakk focused his thoughts: *And that's the crux of the matter, isn't it? We don't have any other viable options. So let's go, but let's be extra careful.*

They rose from their lair and separated. They had developed a system for hunting together and again they put their joint skills into play. As the hunters moved closer to the Ela they reached out to the fragmentary thought patterns of the small forest creatures and the tree dwellers. But instead of helping, these thoughts only added to their own jumbled images. They kept to the southwest, being careful to stay downwind of the herd, whose thoughts continued to come to them more clearly now, but in strange and chaotic fragments, like the lyrics of a song just beyond recognition.

!Kerrt contemplated: *We're close enough that we should be getting better data on the herd. Their thoughts are so…different. I can't even tell how many are in the herd or how many adult males there are.*

I agree, !Zsakk replied. *The thought patterns are unlike any that I've ever experienced, but maybe there's some type of external interference.*

I don't know; it just doesn't feel right, !Kerrt replied to him. *I've never experienced "interference" as you call it,* barely concealing her exasperation. *And the perceptions I read in the minds of the small creatures around us are just as strange. Whatever they are seeing is puzzling to them as well.*

!Zsakk stopped for a minute as he surveyed the cacophony of thoughts in the small minds of the forest creatures. Like !Kerrt he preferred to block out their back ground noise most of the time, but now he needed all the data he could glean.

The visions are very confusing, !Kerrt. But as you pointed out so softly to me earlier, what option do we have? Surely you don't recommend abandoning this hunt. I'm confident that the patterns will be clearer as we get closer, reasoned !Zsakk.

Of course we should continue! I'm no fool; we have little choice, she sneered with bared teeth. *I'm just worried.*

In a way !Zsakk was relieved that she was as apprehensive as he was. He sensed the fear in her mind, but he didn't want to acknowledge or dwell on this. Turning his muzzle upward and sniffing the slight breeze he noted: *We're still downwind of them and I believe they're about a half kilometer away to the northeast.*

The she-panther suddenly turned her face to him and snarled: *I'm not a coward, and you know it! Be careful what you think, male,* she snapped. *Remember that we're close enough that even random stray thoughts can bleed through to each other. I'm just sharing my concerns with you. Don't push our relationship too far!*

!Zsakk felt the real threat in her response. She was a powerful creature, on the edge and could kill him in an instant, if pushed too far. Continuing on both hunters realized they would need to be more careful with their thoughts, given their proximity and the stress on both of them.

Trying as best he could he said: *I'm not questioning your courage, woman and you know this. So let's both just calm down and think about the situation as rationally as possible. As close as we are, you know most of what I am thinking and feeling. I doubt if either of us could hide much at this point. This is another aspect of our relationship that neither of us has any experience with. We need to be more careful around each other, but we also need to get beyond petty squabbling.*

Changing the subject he continued: *I'm sensing more random and more individual thoughts from this herd than I've encountered before. I can't even sense a herd consciousness. And I'm sensing unusual color combinations and odd spatial arrangements in the thoughts of the Ela. What are you sensing?*

Yes, I'm getting the same odd perceptions. I find them... disorienting. The minds of these Ela are certainly different from any I've ever encountered. But we need to get ready. They are still moving toward us and are now no more than three hundred meters away.

The panthers separated to position themselves in an especially thick part of the forest, hoping to reduce defensive maneuvers of the much larger herbivores. The thicker forest also put the Ela at greater disadvantage since they were more dependent on their vision than the hunters.

The herd moved ever closer to the hunters concealed position. !Zsakk used all of his senses to construct an image of the approaching herd and the two hunters. Perhaps it was his concentration on the herd and the tactical situation that distracted him from !Kerrt's thoughts, but he was suddenly aware that she was going to fire her stun pulse into the advancing herd's projected position, despite the fact that neither of them had visualization of a target. He *screamed* at her to hold her fire, but it was too late. Then, almost simultaneously, one of the creatures burst through the brush directly in front of him. As !Kerrt's stun pulse discharged with a flash and a crack, all hell broke loose. There was no time for contemplation or to consider what they were up against. These creatures were definitely not Ela, yet !Zsakk had no option but to fight and support !Kerrt's attack with all his strength. He let his instincts take over discharging his own energy pulse at the creature directly in his view. He saw the creature crumple. !Zsakk dodged quickly behind a tree, focusing all his strength to quickly recharge his storage capacitor as he analyzed the tactical situation and his next target.

He was shocked by another energy discharge off to his left that he thought must signal more of his kind attacking the herd! He quickly focused his mind, searching for *Others* and at the same instant saw an energy beam strike !Kerrt squarely in her chest! He sensed both her surprise and felt her agony. Then he saw additional energy beams strike at her. !Zsakk could find no *Others* to explain the fire engulfing !Kirrt. Then suddenly he realized that the energy beams did not come from one of his kind, but from the strange creatures. The fire came out of sticks they carried! And their fire was incessant, without the need of recharging! Fortunately, there were only two of the small, dangerous creatures left standing and they were hastily retreating into the brush. !Zsakk noted that these creatures ran upright on their two hind legs dodging behind trees to fire their energy beams. They were firing at him now that !Kerrt was down.

As their energy beams lashed the trees and brush around him, !Zsakk aimed another desperate discharge at the devils. "What are these creatures?" he asked himself. And then they were gone, retreated into the forest. "What a disaster," he thought. He frantically searched for the devils' thoughts. But he could read nothing but jumbled and useless perceptions. He knew he was lucky to be alive.

He reached out with his mind searching for !Kerrt. But her mind was silent. He hoped this meant that she was just unconscious, but he was very worried. He made his way cautiously toward her last known position, while constantly scanning the forest for a return of the devils. As he moved through the underbrush, !Kerrt suddenly regained consciousness and her mind screamed out in pain. !Zsakk was shaken by her shriek of anguish that reverberated up and down his spine.

Her pain washed over his mind and he winced from its intensity, almost falling, until he blocked her thoughts. He called to her, but she didn't reply. He realized that she must be seriously injured. He found her lying on her side panting rapidly. Her eyes were glazed and she stared outwardly at nothing. She was in shock. As he assessed her wounds he quickly realized that he had never seen any injury like this before. The energy blasts to her left shoulder, neck, and down her chest had burned away the hair, as well as the flesh down to her shoulder blade. The bone itself was blackened and charred! There was no bleeding; just the gaping hole of destroyed flesh. The smell was awful. !Zsakk was very familiar with the energy burns that his stun pulse could inflict. But this injury was done by a vastly more powerful weapon. He knew instinctively that !Kerrt would not survive this trauma. Her thoughts were increasingly disorganized, explaining why he had been unable to contact her. !Kerrt was dying and there was nothing he could do to change that.

It came to him in a flash that to preserve what he could of her, it would be necessary to absorb !Kerrt like he absorbed an Ela. This was taboo among *Others*, but it was the only way that at least some part of her would stay with him. It came to him that he couldn't just let her slip away. He recognized that his concern about losing her was bizarre, but he felt driven to overcome his revulsion of absorbing !Kerrt. By transferring her essence to him, her thoughts and experiences would be preserved in him; a part of her would become a part of him.

"There's no time for situational ethics, you fool!" he chided himself. "She's dying and if she sinks any lower I won't be able to establish a link." He extended his feeding tongue and hurried to begin the melding process. At first he had difficulty starting the flow of electro-conductive saliva, so dry was his mouth. But thankfully visceral reflexes took over and the electro-conductive drool began to flow. The neuro-electrical connection was also difficult through the charred and denuded flesh, but he finally established a good connection to her nervous system. His mind extended frantically along her damaged peripheral nervous system seeking her spinal cord and her brain. He felt the excruciating pain that she was experiencing and forced himself to maintain contact. As the waves of pain washed over him he asked abstractly, "Why am I doing this? Why would I choose to suffer for another? Where did this urge come from?" He would have never considered absorbing !Kerrt without their closeness from the recent past. He watched her life force moving away from her dying body as it began to move into his mind. He suddenly imagined that he was observing himself next to !Kerrt's body from a high vantage point. At times he wondered whether he would lose himself or his mind as he attempted to save her soul. The vision from above suddenly merged with him and he was alone next to her dead body. "Is it...*love* that drives me to endure this horror?"

Emotions flooded his consciousness as her energy flowed into him. He felt and saw her essence, her soul, *pass* by him, as if he were standing by a trail and watching someone pass by. She *looked* at him and *touched* him as she moved through him ever so slowly. Their *joining* was the most intense experience of his life. He glimpsed the panoply of her thoughts and her life's experiences. No longer was the perspective from the outside or above, but one of a shared vision. The experience was at once sensual and spiritual. *Oh !Kerrt,* he sighed as he saw and felt her engrams overlaid upon his own. She was a part of him now. He had assimilated another sentient being, his partner, the only being to whom he had ever been close.

He sat there stunned for a moment, considering what he had just experienced and the nature of his kind. "Absorbing the tiny forest creatures or Ela was so different," he thought. Though he honored the creatures he killed, he had never experienced anything like the absorption of !Kerrt. He rationalized that these other beings weren't really thoughtful creatures like *Others*. Consequently, there had never been any sense of remorse, just the bloodlust of the kill and the luxurious flow of neural energy draining from his prey. But now he wondered about these other creatures. "Did they feel in some small way like !Kerrt when they died?" And he saw something in !Kerrt's mind as she merged with him. Yes there was a sense of sadness when she realized that she was dying; but there was also something more, something just on the edge of her thoughts. !Zsakk saw in her thoughts a sense of peace and then at the instant of her death, he saw through her eyes an intense and indescribable vision of light! "How strange," he thought to himself.

He shook himself out of his daydream, retracted his tongue and again scanned the area for the enemy. "Philosophical musings are going to get you killed, you fool," he chided himself. And what was getting into him anyway? Why was he thinking like this? Concern about !Kerrt he could understand, but concerns about Ela were just bizarre. "After all, I've just fought a pitched battle, lost !Kerrt and absorbed an *Other*!" he shuddered. "Don't go pansy ass, !Zsakk, worrying about Ela, for God's sake! You've got to eat to live. You either hunt or die. This was the way of things. It has always been this way." His troubled mind worked furiously as he carefully and respectfully separated himself from "his" !Kerrt, whose body was now dead, but whose soul he carried within his mind and his heart.

He again sensed the distant and strange thoughts of the two legged beings. He could now recognize their minds, even though he couldn't make much sense of their thoughts. "They must have run far away by now," he thought. But then he thought again, "What if they can shield their minds from me? We didn't sense their nature until it was too late, my !Kerrt," he lamented. "Who knows what these creatures are capable of?"

He cautiously moved toward the closest of the stunned alien creatures. As he stood over the strange small creature that was paralyzed, yet conscious, !Zsakk sensed fear in the being. But he also saw a mind that was under control and was calculating, looking for an opportunity to attack him. This was no ordinary creature. It was intelligent and very dangerous.

What are you? he bellowed at the creature with his thoughts. *Where did you come from? You killed my mate!* he screamed with all his savagery. It was difficult to control his rage at the impotent being beneath his forepaw. *I should just kill you and then leave this cursed place,* he roared.

There was no response from the being's mind. *It's curious that I'm unable to penetrate your mind, Ela, or whatever you are,* he said with a snarl. *You won't give me your secrets? Well, then I will take them, and my !Kerrt's death will count for something. I will have you slowly and painfully, Ela, since you resist me, and then I will have answers to my questions!*

He extended his feeding tongue and roughly stabbed the creature's neck with the pointed tip. He smiled as he watched the creature flinch with pain and fear as he started the melding process. As contact was made, the creature's thoughts began to wash over his consciousness and he was shocked to see how developed its mind was and what a vast store of neural energy it contained.

You truly are an unusual creature, he thought at the being. He wondered for an instant whether the energy patterns could be poisonous to him. But the photons *tasted* okay and he felt the knowledge he would gain justified the theoretical risk of absorbing such an alien mind. He surprised himself when he transiently thought, "Is it right to absorb and kill this intelligent creature? What's got into you, !Zsakk? Kill the little shit!" He quickly suppressed this strange concept of empathy directed at something so loathsome that had killed his !Kerrt. He wondered, "What would make me have such a ridiculous thought anyway?"

Perhaps it was the slight turning of his head, as he considered the alien, which saved him. An energy beam struck the tree behind !Zsakk and with a loud crack the energy evaporated the moisture of the tree, exploding it. He ducked instinctively, quickly retracting his feeding tongue severing the connection with the creature.

He thought, "The two aliens have come back and I was unaware of them until the attack!" Was he just distracted and made clumsy by his anger? Another thought dawned on him. "Could I have been distracted by the creature and made to overlook the returning devils?" He had never known Ela to return to help an injured or fallen member of their herd; and yet these dangerous creatures had returned to attack him! "Perhaps my emotions are clouding my judgment," he thought. "I've got to get out of here or they'll kill me!"

There was no time for further analysis. He leapt over an intervening log and bounded into the relative safety of the dense forest. "I've got to put some distance between me and these devils. Oh !Kerrt, I am alone again!" he thought as he wove a serpentine path through the trees to hopefully not give the aliens a clear shot at him. "I never realized my loneliness till I lost you." Waves of self pity swept over him as he ran for his life, ever farther from the broken body of his !Kerrt. He steeled himself to the pain of loss, consoling himself with the knowledge that he now carried her essence in his mind and in his heart. "I will never forget you, !Kerrt. I will think of you when I see the lights in the sky each night!"

CHAPTER 16

Beta Continent

Cooper was pretty sure he had hit one of the beasts with his plasma rifle. The pained howl of the creature confirmed his suspicion. However, he had been so busy getting Snyder down that his other shots were probably little more than covering fire. He knew that any hit with a plasma beam would likely result in significant injury. The molten fire of a plasma beam tended to cling to any surface, transmitting its substantial energy with lethal efficiency. "They may be big," he sneered, "but a plasma beam will melt flesh."

He thought tactically as he literally drug Snyder back through the undergrowth. There must have been at least two attackers, since there had been two lines of fire coming from both sides of the trail they had been following. He thought that the aliens' energy bursts were similar to a lightening flash and might be an electrical discharge.

"Doc!" he huffed. "Did you see any weapons on those cats?"

Jenny Snyder was scared to death. She was a scientist for heaven's sakes! And now she found herself being literally drug through the bush by her shirt collar, and a marine is asking her a military question. "How the hell do I know, Sergeant?" she screamed with as much indignation as she could muster. "Let go of my collar and give me a chance to stand up and walk."

He let go of her collar but grabbed her arm, wrenching it downward as she struggled to stand up. "Don't stand up, Jenny, or those cats may fry your ass! I have people down and I don't want to lose you too," said Cooper. "I believe their weapon is like an electrical discharge; probably not as effective as a plasma rifle, but potentially just as deadly."

They again moved through the brush, this time in a crouched single file with Cooper leading. A tree branch swung backward and hit Snyder squarely in the face and she fell backwards with a cry. Cooper turned and tried to help her up, but she just as quickly jerked her arm indignantly away from his helping hand.

"Get your hands off me, Sergeant!"

He quickly scanned the surroundings and then said quietly, but in a commanding voice, "Listen, Dr. Snyder, we're in deep shit. We've got injured people down, we're in a war zone and we're not gonna get help anytime soon. I don't have time to soothe feelings. I pulled you down before you got yourself shot. I'm in charge of what's left of this outfit and I need your help, not your lip or a pout. And I need you to follow my orders. Do you understand?"

"Perfectly!" she hissed, dabbing at the small cut over her left eye. "I'm not a soldier, but I'm not a fool either."

He scanned the brush again and then made eye contact with the frustrated scientist, "No Ma'am, you're not a fool; but you are in the marines now. If we work together we might get out of this mess alive and get back to help our guys. Now what's your opinion of their weapon?"

"I told you, Sergeant, I don't know! The flash was out of the corner of my eye, but I guess it could have been an electrical discharge. The thunder clap would be consistent with expanding superheated water vapor that occurs in a lightening discharge. If this is correct we're talking about millions of volts. I never saw a weapon, but everything happened so fast I'm not sure of anything."

Cooper was glad to see Snyder transition to her analytical self and control her fear. "I never saw one either, Doc. Do you think it would be possible for an animal to generate and store that degree of electrical energy?"

"It hardly seems likely, but the moray eel on Earth can generate and deliver an electrical shock. We're fifty light-years from home and who knows what nature is capable of here."

"That's a good point. And… thanks for getting down, Doc. I'd be real sad if a kitty fried you."

"I'll take that as a genuine pleasantry, Sergeant. And I'm sorry about my attitude; I've never been shot at before. And I've never been drug through the jungle by my shirt collar either; it just got me a bit irritated."

Cooper managed a slight nod and a muffled, "Humph."

They stopped about hundred meters back down the trail, away from the noise, smoke, and confusion of the firefight. Cooper called to the downed team members on the con link but was not surprised when he got no response. In a firefight with ionized plasma fire and perhaps high voltage electricity there was bound to be a temporary disruption of any electromagnetic based communication system. And he had to also consider that Hinton and Grieve were captured, unconscious, or dead. A grim thought he realized, but a realistic one. He knew that Grieve was on point at the moment of the attack and was pretty sure he had been hit; Cooper had seen him crumple and fall. He also thought that Hinton had been hit, but in the confusion of the fire fight the Commander may have just dove for cover.

They slipped from the path and moved into the surrounding brush, crouching behind a fallen tree that afforded them some cover and a view of the trail. Cooper readied himself for the attack that he felt would come soon. He wondered if they could survive another assault. "Hell, half the team was down in the first encounter with these sons of bitches!" he cursed softly.

"Cover the damn trail with your laser pistol, Doc!" he ordered. "Those assholes will be coming soon to finish the business they started. Here, point the weapon toward that bend in the trail and keep your head down," he hissed.

Snyder dutifully obeyed the experienced marine, but it was obvious to Cooper that Snyder could not be expected to do much damage with her light side arm and her inexperience.

"May Day! May Day! We are under attack by hostiles," he signaled over the broad band channel that he hoped would be received at the landing boat. "Two members of our team are down, including Commander Hinton. Come in landing craft," whispered Cooper into his com-link.

"Pilot Wise here," returned the static filled reply. "I copy your situation. We've been trying to contact you since we registered weapons' discharges seven minutes ago. I can see your position by the GPS. I don't see how I can land the boat near you since the forest is far too thick there."

"I agree," said Cooper, just glad to hear someone else's voice. "Also, our tactical situation is not good and I wouldn't risk bringing you here at this time. We don't know who or what attacked us and we don't know their strength. I saw at least one large quadruped that had some type of energy weapon. We're about one hundred meters from where we were attacked and we'll stay in this position for a few more minutes. I'm preparing for another attack from the aliens, but perhaps we bloodied their noses enough that they retreated to regroup. Dr. Snyder is with me and neither of us is injured. If we're not attacked in the next few minutes we'll try to double back and attempt to find Commander Hinton and Private Grieve."

Cooper studied the relayed GPS data on his tactical hand-held interface as he repeatedly glanced up to survey the trail. He continued his planning aloud so that the boat and Snyder would all be on the same page.

"The GPS shows us about three kilometers from the boat. I want you to track our signals as we move. Also make sure *Odyssey* knows our status. If we don't check in with you in thirty minutes consider us lost and take the boat back to the ship. You'll be able to pinpointe the locations of our energy weapons' discharge, so you'll be able find our last position even if we are hit. Do not attempt to aid us without reinforcements from the ship or my authorization. Do you copy?"

"Roger your plan. I'll communicate with *Odyssey* and get the rest of our people back into the boat as a defensive measure. Good luck, Sergeant."

"Yeah, we'll need it" Cooper muttered. "Survey team out."

"Sergeant, why didn't you get us some back up?" pleaded Snyder. "We need help! We've just been attacked and two of our team may be dead! I don't have any military experience and I barely know how to fire my laser pistol."

"Keep your voice down, Doc! The boat can't land here. We're on our own for right now. I want you to at least lay down covering fire when they come."

"But Sarge…"

"Shut up, Doc!" he said under his breath, but with as much venom as he could muster. "We're in a bad way here. I need your help. I don't want any whining. Now you either do as I say or I'll leave you here in the forest. I don't have time to debate the situation or the plan. Now get up and move ten meters to my right. I want you to stay low, move quietly and don't shoot at anything that you can't see. I don't want any friendly fire casualties in case the Commander or Private Grieve comes down that trail. As I told the boat, if the aliens don't hit us in the next few minutes, we'll move slowly back up the trail to where we were attacked and look for our mates. Any questions?" he growled as he looked her straight in her eyes.

The scientist slowly shook her head. "Sergeant Cooper, I'm scared… shitless."

Cooper noted her lapse into coarse language, as a sure sign of fear. "Me too, Jenny," he said softly as he looked left and right along the trail. "Combat is always this way. You never get used to the fear. The best thing you can do is stay focused on your job. Now let's get ready to move out if the buggers don't hit us again soon."

It was a long ten minutes, but there was no attack or sign of the aliens. Likewise they saw and heard nothing during the short march back to the skirmish site. The forest was menacingly quiet. "Perhaps this is a good sign," Cooper hoped to himself, but he realized the aliens may be counting on their return and could be laying in ambush again.

The attack zone was easy to see due to smoke from the smoldering brush that had been burned by the plasma discharges. The air was heavy and smelled of ozone and burned flesh, Cooper noted with a sickened realization.

Snyder was the first to see the great panther-like creature. She turned to Cooper and pointed excitedly at the beast. Cooper estimated that it stood at least two meters at its shoulders and was jet black in color. There didn't seem to be any other creatures around and it seemed to be preoccupied with something at its feet.

Cooper quickly decided to take a shot at the creature and not risk a closer approach. He knew his plasma rifle's arc of fire would need to be tight to avoid igniting the intervening brush and dissipating the beam's power. The only trouble was that a plasma rifle was not accurate at this distance, but it was the best they had. He didn't think the more accurate laser pistol would be powerful enough to knock the beast down or kill it without an extremely lucky head or heart shot. "Besides this creature might have its heart in its ass for all I know," he muttered while adjusting the rifle's settings.

Cooper took aim and fired. He saw the beam pass over the alien's crouched torso, missing the creature by only a few centimeters. The beam hit a tree immediately behind the panther, exploding it. The tree came crashing down all around the panther. Under the cover of the explosion and the crashing tree the alien disappeared amazingly fast into the forest, apparently uninjured.

Snyder also shot at the beast with her laser pistol, but it was already gone. There was no return fire from the alien or any of its comrades, so Cooper concluded that it was alone. But he was sure there had been two lines of fire with the initial attack. So where were the other aliens?

He and Snyder moved forward cautiously and first came upon Grieve. Cooper saw that he was dead. The alien's weapon had apparently struck the private in the chest, perhaps electrocuting him. There was some charred clothing, but no overt tissue destruction like a plasma weapon caused. They next found the alien Cooper hit with his plasma rifle during the firefight. It was also dead from apparent massive tissue damage caused by the powerful plasma beam.

"At least we know we can kill the damn things," said Cooper. "And this explains the two lines of fire; there must have just been two of them."

Cooper noted that under these circumstances not even Snyder was interested in any analysis of the creature other than the assurance that the alien was dead, its three glassy eyes staring upward into nothing.

"I found the Commander!" cried Snyder. "He's alive, but he's unconscious!"

Cooper crossed the clearing to Snyder's side. "Yeah, but just barely alive," grunted Cooper, as he felt Hinton's weak and thready pulse. He had seen battle injuries many times and he knew they needed to get some fluids into the Commander if he were to have a chance.

"He's in shock. Break open your med kit, Doc; it should be in your rucksack. I'll try to get a line in him to give him some fluids. And keep your eyes open for that damned monster."

Hinton was more fortunate than Private Grieve. Perhaps Hinton received a less intense energy bolt or the full energy of the blast was deflected. From the electrical burn pattern it looked to Cooper that the Commander had been struck in the upper arm and shoulder. "Maybe a hit outside the chest is what saved him," Cooper thought to himself, as he worked on getting a line in and the fluids going. Whatever the reason, the Commander was alive, but breathing with shallow rapid respirations and moaning softly. He did not respond to them even as they gently rolled him over to further assess the extent of his trauma.

"What's that?" asked Snyder when she noted what looked like a small hole at the side of Hinton's neck. The area was oozing a small amount of blood and was covered with what looked like a large amount of a thick clear slime.

"I don't know," said Cooper as he wiped away the slime. He put his finger up to his nose and smelled the gooey stuff. "There's a musky smell to it. Here, what do you think?"

Snyder flinched. "Get that away from my face and yours! You have no idea what that is. The alien was right here beside the Commander and that stuff could be some sort of body fluid or even saliva!"

Cooper wiped his hand off on his coveralls and said, "You're right, Doc. We don't need to take any chances or assume anything. We've both been through a tough day on foreign soil, to say the least. Let's get some antibiotics in the Commander and bolus him with some

JAMES Y. FERGUSON M.D.

pressors. We'll have to improvise a stretcher and carry him to the forest's edge."

"Corporal Green, can you hear me?" radioed Cooper.

"Yeah, Tom. It's great to hear from you! What's your status?"

"Grieve is dead. The Commander is seriously wounded and in shock. We're attempting to stabilize his condition. We drove off the only other alien we saw. There was no other attack. We're fashioning a litter for the Commander and we'll begin moving back down the trail soon. We'll meet you at the forest's edge as soon as we can get there. I want you to move the boat closer to the forest's edge and wait for us there."

"Sergeant Cooper, this is acting Captain Woolsey on *Odyssey*. I'm following your progress and I agree with your plans. How long will it take you to get back to the forest edge?"

"Probably an hour and a half, Sir, unless we have additional problems. I'll call if we get slowed down."

"Roger. God speed, Sergeant."

They took turns pulling the litter while the other one covered their rear with the plasma rifle. They were forced to leave Grieve behind out of practicality. Cooper silently promised his fallen shipmate, "We'll be back for you soon, David."

During the difficult march back they were under constant fear of attack. It was necessary for Cooper to do most of the portage, but he noted that Jenny showed great concentration and courage in covering the forest for hostiles. Cooper thought to himself how combat promotes maturity. As Cooper struggled to drag the litter through the thick jungle, he allowed himself the occasional pitiable thought, "It's been a long, tough day Coop—perhaps the longest day of my life."

CHAPTER 17

There is a tide in the affairs of men which, taken at the flood leads
on to fortune; omitted, all the voyage of their life is bound in
shallows and miseries. We must take the current when it serves or
lose our ventures.

SHAKESPEARE from
Julius Caesar

Alpha Continent

Havel slowly approached the creature. Its appearance was so like a
mythological faun that it was enchanting. It had assumed a squatting
position on its hind legs with its arms crossed and just stared at them
like the Cheshire Cat. Its body language was relaxed as if the creature
was in control of the situation after all.

Havel concentrated on keeping his hands outstretched, his
arms relaxed and his palms up. He had no idea whether these were the
right gestures, but it just seemed appropriate and non-threatening; he
was counting on his instincts.

Havel reassuringly sensed Walker following a few paces
behind him. They both stopped about ten meters from the alien and
Havel heard himself repeat the same corny hello, this time more self-
consciously. Again there was no response from the alien, other than an
intense stare from the deeply yellow eyes in the midline of its triangular
face. The alien's only movement was to direct his ears toward them
and again to tilt its head ever so slightly. Havel thought this gesture

was cute when his dog did it; he wasn't so sure the alien's head tilt was cute.

The three of them stood there observing each another. Havel observed the creature's two powerful hind legs that seemed to be similar to a human's. But instead of feet, the alien had hoof-like extensions of its legs. The creature's body was covered in short cropped hair that had a definite iridescent tint. It wore very lightweight and loose clothing over its lower torso and wore a tunic to its waist. The large triangular head had an ovoid mouth-like opening without any lips.

"Bill, I don't know why, but I believe that our friend understands what we're doing. I think this big guy is highly intelligent or he would have run off the minute he saw us. But, hell, what do we know?"

"Not much, Captain," whispered Walker.

On a whim Havel concentrated intensely on the alien, looking him straight in its strange, apical eye. He concentrated on forming his words in his mind slowly and deliberately: *We're strangers from far away and we mean you no harm.*

The creature reacted immediately, cocking its head again and pointing its ears directly at Havel. At the same time the alien wrinkled its brow in what looked like an expression of surprise.

Havel heard Walker start to comment on the alien's response so he raised his hand emphatically and whispered, "Quiet, Bill. Concentrate on the alien and listen." Within an instant Havel was bombarded with a burst of perceptions, thoughts, and feelings. The impressions were so powerful that Havel felt his knees almost give way and he slumped slightly.

"Captain, are you alright?" He felt Walker's hand on his arm steadying him, but Havel waved him off and straightened himself.

"I'm alright, Bill. Did you sense anything just then?"

"Just some vague perceptions, Captain. I didn't hear anything though."

"Bill, I know this may sound crazy, but I think our friend is telepathic and is trying to communicate with me! Everyone, be still and don't distract me or the alien." Havel quickly returned his gaze to the alien and focused his thoughts: *You must make your thoughts slowly. We don't communicate like you and aren't accustomed to your ways.*

This time the alien's thoughts were more concrete and to the point. *What are you? I saw something strange in the sky this morning and I come here and find even stranger things.*

Despite the extraordinary interaction and the alien's strange perceptions, Havel found that he was able to understand the alien, as long as the creature "thought" slowly.

Havel responded to the alien: *We call ourselves humans and we're explorers. We didn't want to disturb you so we stayed far from your village. It's against our rules to interfere with others, but we would like to know you and learn from you.*

Tenge considered the human's thoughts. Their minds and thoughts patterns were very different and this lent credibility to the human's story, even though it was quite extraordinary. But how else could one explain the sky-boat and these strange two-legged beings that can reason like the People?

I'm called Tenge. We call ourselves the People.

Havel continued, finding the process of forming and directing his words easier with practice. *We have never encountered a being as thoughtful as you or one who can speak with his mind. We speak with our mouths*, returned Havel, pointing to his lips.

Tenge responded: *Our children speak with their mouths before their Awakening. What do you call yourself? And where is the place you come from?*

My name is Captain James Havel and these humans are my crew members, he projected, gesturing to Walker and the others behind him. *It may be hard for you to imagine, but we come from another world that circles one of the twinkling stars that you see at night.*

Havel's statement hit Tenge like a brick in the face! This declaration was even more astounding than the sky-boat or these strange beings. If this were true, it was a validation of all that he had imagined for so long. He uttered a silent prayer to the Maker for allowing him to be the one who was picked to meet these travelers.

Tenge telepathed: *I have thought about the possibility of other places all of my life, but I'm a bit different from others in my village. It is fortunate that I am the first one to meet you. Some of my People will be scared by what you say, and I'm a bit shaken as well. It will take me awhile to consider your words. There is much to do before our peoples can meet. I need to return to my village now and prepare my People. I will come back tomorrow and we can "speak" again. If you are an honorable being you will stay here until I return. I will try to bring some of the Elders of my village with me tomorrow.*

Again Havel was amazed by Tenge's composure and more so by his logic. He thought to himself, "These may be technologically unsophisticated beings, but they are otherwise very advanced."

We agree to your suggestion, Tenge. You have my word that we'll abide by your wishes and remain here. I look forward to "speaking" with you again.

"Bill, give me your recorder." Taking the device from the puzzled linguist, Havel turned back to Tenge and concentrated: *I'd like you to take this recording device with you. If you push this button you can hear our voices. If you want to show this to your Elders it may make them curious enough to come back with you and meet us.*

Thank you, Captain. You are wise. I will take your talking box with me. This may indeed encourage some to come because we certainly have nothing like this. Good bye until tomorrow.

The alien stood up and quickly trotted to the forest's edge and then disappeared without looking back.

"Holy shit!" exploded Walker. "What was all that about? Were you really... communicating with the creature? I kept sensing things, but I couldn't pick up anything specific."

"Bill, this is perhaps the greatest discovery of our time. We've made contact with an advanced species and I was able to communicate with them telepathically! They call themselves the People and our satyr, or faun, or what ever it is, calls himself, Tenge. He says he'll come back tomorrow, and hopefully bring some of the villagers with him."

"This is incredible, Captain! I really don't know what to say. How did you start...talking to him? I saw his head turn toward you and then you almost stumbled."

"I just got a hunch from the perceptions we were all having. So I just concentrated all my thoughts on him and formed the words in my mind. It's kind of like the difference between having a thought and seeing the thoughts as words. I don't understand what happened, but I guess it worked."

"Worked? That's the biggest understatement I've ever heard! Captain, do you realize what this could mean? The People might be able to show us the way to a new level of communication and interaction. Humanity could go 'virtual!' Wait till I report this to Dr. Tapp. You know her group on Earth has been working on higher brain function. They've been exploring the possibility of telepathic communication in animals for years."

"Yes, I know about the good doctor's work. And this does raise many possibilities. But more important than anything else, Bill, we aren't alone in the universe!"

CHAPTER 13

A foolish consistency is the hobgoblin of little minds.
RALPH WALDO EMERSON

Beta Continent

The trek back to the landing craft was a struggle, physically and emotionally. Dragging Hinton on the makeshift stretcher through the forest was exhausting work, and at any instant Cooper expected an ambush. But an attack never came. Hinton remained unresponsive and just groaned as he bounced along over the uneven ground. Under the direction of Dr. Tapp on *Odyssey*, Snyder had done a good job keeping Hinton's blood pressure up with pressors and treating his burn wounds.

After their struggles the flight back to *Odyssey* was anticlimactic for Cooper and Snyder. With the last of his strength, Cooper dutifully endured the arduous debriefing that began as soon as the landing craft lifted off. Snyder did a field Nuclear Magnetic Resonance scan of Hinton as soon as they got him on the boat and those results were sent ahead to the crash team awaiting them on *Odyssey*.

Dr. Tapp and her medical team were ready for them in *Odyssey*'s docking bay. Cooper and Snyder stood back as the crash team took over and transported Hinton, with IV's dangling like Christmas ornaments from his gurney, to the medical suite. Even as the elevator doors were closing Lieutenant Woolsey began peppering them with more questions about the attack and their observations.

"Sir, with all due respect, Dr. Snyder and I have told you all we can remember at this moment," said Cooper. "We're exhausted. Maybe with some rest we can be more helpful. Dr. Snyder did some superficial scans of the alien as I was cutting saplings for the litter. She sent the scan data up to the ship as we were achieving orbit. I hope the data helps us to understand the creatures. The Doc and I both feel that they are intelligent and obviously dangerous. The attack was a coordinated effort, like a pack of wolves. I can't comment on whether it's more than just an advanced predator. Maybe Jenny would have a better perspective on this. We never found any weapons; perhaps they generate the electrical pulse and use it as a weapon. Whatever the science boys decide, I know that we're in for a tough time if we go back into its territory."

"Oh, we'll be going back down, Sergeant, but this time in force," said Woolsey with conviction. "We've got to recover Mr. Grieve's body and we'll need to study the dead alien in detail. And rest assured, we'll be going back with armor this time.

But thank you again, Tom, for bringing your team out and saving the Commander," continued Woolsey. "I know you're both exhausted. Get a shower, some chow, and some rest, but I want your full report by 0800 hours tomorrow. You did a good job down there soldier. I hope Commander Hinton will be able to thank you both in person soon. And Jenny, perhaps you've got some marine in you after all."

"I don't think so, John," the weary Snyder mumbled.

"I'll be in touch with Captain Havel again soon," said Woolsey. "Dismissed, Sergeant."

The marine said, "Thank you, Sir, and... good watch," saluting automatically.

Woolsey could literally feel the fatigue in Cooper's voice and see it in both of them as he watched Cooper and Snyder exit the landing bay.

Woolsey hurried to catch up with the crash team transporting Hinton to the medical suite. As he took an elevator down-ship, he began forming his next update for the Captain. The Alpha team had also encountered intelligent aliens, but there had been no signs of the panther-like creatures that had attacked the Beta Team. Nonetheless, everyone was extremely wary.

As the lift door opened on the Medical Deck, Woolsey was greeted by hordes of people milling around in the hall outside the medical suite and shouts from inside the clinic. As Woolsey cut his way through and reached the doorway of the medical suite, Dr. Tapp cast a sideways glance at him and without interrupting her efforts said, "Lieutenant Woolsey, that's far enough. My people and I are very busy. We don't have anything to report to you at this time. Please leave us to our business and when we know something, I'll call you."

"Understood, doctor. I don't think I'll be in anyone's way if I stand here in the doorway. I need to make some kind of announcement to the crew; they know of the attack and Private Grieve's death. Everyone is worried about the Commander and it'll help if I update them as soon as possible. I've already briefed the Captain on what we know so far."

Without looking up or interrupting her work on Hinton, Tapp asked, "How soon will the Alpha team be back on board?"

"It may be awhile, Doc. They're making progress on Alpha," said Woolsey.

She looked up and asked incredulously, "Do you mean Alpha is not on the way back to *Odyssey*?"

"That's correct, Doctor. The Captain and his team made contact with an intelligent species and there are plans for more interaction with these aliens in the morning."

"Damnation, Lieutenant!" Tapp exploded. "We've been attacked, we've lost a comrade and another one's life hangs in the balance. Don't you think prudence should dictate? Forgive the mother in me, but we should get all the children home right now! How do we know that this other species is not equally dangerous to the Alpha Team?"

Woolsey was glad that he was still in the doorway and that Tapp couldn't physically reach him. He envisioned being grabbed by the ear as his grade school teacher used to do when he misbehaved. Tapp continued to mumble her displeasure as she examined Hinton's belly, repeatedly glancing up to study the data readouts above his bed.

Woolsey continued, "In some ways I agree with you, Dr. Tapp, but I trust the Captain's judgment; he knows what he's doing. And there isn't much he could do here to help the Commander. This is a job for you and your staff. I'm sure the Captain knows this and feels the risks are justified. At any rate, it's his call."

"Humph!" was all Woolsey could hear Tapp mutter contemptuously under her breath.

"Dr. Tapp, look at these readings!" came the excited response of Med-Surg specialist Lu Farmer. "I'm recalibrating the equipment before I take another reading, but the data suggests that the Commander's presynaptic membranes have been severely depleted of neurotransmitters."

"Hmm...," said Tapp, as she studied the real time data monitors. "Perhaps the energy burst did this, but I've never heard of an electrocution causing this kind of injury. Recalibrate and run the scan again, Lu," said Tapp. "We obviously have no experience with this type of trauma. Perhaps our theory of an electrical pulse is wrong. This depletion of neuro transmitters may be an important clue to the weapon system of the aliens."

At the mention of weapons, Woolsey asked from the doorway, "Does that mean he wasn't shot with an electrical energy beam?"

"Lieutenant, I've tried to be respectful of you and your job, but I want you out of here now. If I have to, I'll throw your ass out myself. I told you we don't know anything yet. Feel free to monitor us on video and audio, but for now get out of my 'ER'!"

Tapp slammed the entrance door in the retreating Woolsey's face and then moved to stand next to her nurse as the repeat scan data began to be displayed on the monitors. Tapp scanned the data and speaking loudly enough to include everyone, "I believe you're right, Lu. There is considerable disruption at the presynaptic membranes. But the entire nervous system has been damaged as well. And this data suggests that the brain and spinal chord injuries are different than the dysfunction at the neuronal synaptic clefts in the peripheral nervous system. Look at the EEG pattern," Tapp continued thinking out loud so as to include her entire staff in the evaluation and treatment process. "The pattern is somewhat similar to what I've seen after an induced seizure from *electroconvulsive therapy.* Perhaps the combination of shock and neuro transmitter depletion is sufficient to explain the clinical situation."

"That would account for his altered central nervous system status," said Farmer. She turned her head slightly and caught the eye of Tech Specialist MaryAnn Sams standing on the other side of Hinton's bed. Sams nodded toward Tapp, as they shared an inside joke about Dr. Tapp's peculiar habit of placing her left hand on her chin when she was lost in thought. Sams had been the first to observe this little idiosyncrasy and initiate their inside joke.

Sams and Farmer spent a lot of time observing and treating the crew's aches and pains. They loved to find the "little quirks that make us all unique." "The Doc just goes into a world of her own when that left hand goes to her chin. And when the index finger separates and goes up over her lips, watch out! It usually means work is coming our way. I can hear her brain humming when she gets philosophical," said MaryAnn.

They watched as Tapp's hand came down from its "contemplative" position. She said, "Well, perhaps you're right Lu, but let's run another MRI sequence along with an NMR spectrographic analysis. MaryAnn, I want to set up a real time PET scan to analyze his brain's metabolic activity."

"It'll take about five minutes to set up the deoxyglucose infusion and the PET scan, Dr. Tapp; but I'm on it," said Sams.

"It'll take several minutes for the repeat MRI and SPEC scans as well," said Farmer, turning to restart the scanning sequence.

As she waited for the data to arrive, Tapp thought back to her training years, running resuscitations in the middle of the night on critically ill patients. If you had a technical job you could lose yourself in the task and not think about the person. She didn't have that option here because she was the highest ranking medical officer on the Ship. "If I screw up or miss something, the Commander might not make it," she sighed inwardly. She was supposed to know what to do, but she realized that often in a medical crisis all you had to go on was your best scientific guess, experience, or gut feelings.

She watched her team working feverishly over the Commander, their crew mate, "and all of us so far from home," she sighed. She caught her reflection in the monitor as she stared at the data stream.

"I've got to quit rubbing my chin when I'm thinking," she thought. "I look like that damn chimp holding Darwin's skull in contemplation."

Her momentary reflections were broken as Sams called out, "Scans completed; the data is streaming."

Tapp reviewed the images, again thinking out loud. "The MRI and SPEC changes look bad, but seem discordant with the PET data. The PET indicates that his brain is very metabolically active. So why has the Commander slipped back into a coma since getting back to the ship?

MaryAnn, give me the first SPEC numbers again."

Tapp studied and compared the two sets of data. "This is looking bad, people. The SPEC data shows a further 15% decline in neuropeptide levels from just twenty minutes ago. Folks, we're going to lose the Commander if this trend continues and we can't reverse the falling peptides. These peptides allow neurons to transmit neural signals enabling us to think and move. Without neural energy exchange, we die," said Tapp with tension and a certain degree of resignation in her voice.

"Lu, I want to give him a three hundred microgram infusion of neurotransmitter precursors as quickly as possible."

"Which ones, Dr. Tapp?"

"All six classes and the subtypes as well, Lu."

And as an after thought, Tapp said, "And MaryAnn, give the Commander two hundred micrograms of Neurotropin as soon as the neurotransmitters are infusing."

Sams glanced quickly at Farmer and then back at Tapp. This was not so much as a challenge of the doctor's authority, but to reassure herself that she had understood the doctor correctly. She had seen doctors in a crisis make errors in the doses of meds. It was a credit to Tapp that Sams felt comfortable enough to ask for clarification, even though it was her professional responsibility to question any order that seemed unusual.

"Dr. Tapp, you do realize that two hundred micrograms of Neurotropin is ten times the standard dose of this agent."

"Yes, I realize that, MaryAnn," said Tapp softly. "But I believe we have one chance of turning this situation around; we won't get a second chance. The neural links in his nervous system are breaking down and he is going to die unless we do something radical."

Sams and Farmer nodded their heads and quickly prepared the neural stimulating cocktails, thankful that they didn't have the responsibility for making the call.

As Farmer began the neurotransmitter infusion through a central line, Sams gave the Neurotropin IV push. Everyone could read the worry in Tapp's demeanor and recognize the desperation in her therapy. They had all seen neural trauma and knew that last-ditch resuscitative efforts rarely worked and often only delayed the inevitable. Tapp had used this cocktail in her work on Earth in neuro-genesis experiments on the enhancement of synaptic brain connections of animals. If Hinton were deficient in presynaptic neurotransmitters, which enabled neurons to exchange information with each other, then she reasoned that she should try to replace this apparent deficiency. A gut feeling told her to give the Neurotropin concomitantly in an attempt to reintegrate the peripheral and central nervous system functions that were unraveling. She was flying by the seat of her pants and she knew it; they all knew it.

Of course, no one had treated someone with Hinton's type of injury. Their treatments for electrical injury had helped somewhat, but Tapp was sure they were not getting at the underlying problem. Tapp searched her mind and clinical experience for other options as she watched her patient slipping away.

"The presynaptic vesicles are showing some signs of repletion, Doctor. And the Commander's heart rate and blood pressure are less erratic over the last five minutes," said Farmer scanning the monitors.

"Thanks, Lu. Please give the Commander another 25 microgram bolus of Neurotropin."

"Yes, Sir," said Farmer.

Tapp studied the real time Electroencephalogram and the NMR spectrographic and PET read outs. Hinton's brain activity was furious and the peripheral nervous system deficits were improving. "So why wasn't he waking up?" she wondered. He was still comatose with only purposeless twitches of his muscles that the EEG told her were not due to seizures. "The muscles are just effectively disconnected from their neurons," she surmised. Not a healthy state or a sustainable one, Tapp knew.

It was moments like these that Tapp wished she had someone else to help her with grave decisions. Everyone looked to her for direction and she didn't really know what else to do. It was a helpless feeling when you've done everything and that wasn't enough. For the first time she admitted to herself, "I'm going to lose him, my patient, my friend." She wracked her brain for anything else that might save him, or "spare me the pain I'll feel when he dies. I understand why some choose careers that avoid emergency life and death decisions. Maybe I should have stayed on Earth," she sighed.

"There doesn't seem to be any reintegration of the peripheral and central nervous system, Dr. Tapp," said Farmer. "And it looks like the neurotransmitter levels are beginning to fall again."

Nurse Farmer's report brought Tapp back from her personal *pity party*. "It's time to put your big girl panties on Helen," she mumbled to herself.

"OK, Ms. Sams," said Tapp, "give the Commander 15 milligrams of thallium IV push. Then go into my office and get the neuro-cortical stimulator. You'll find it in the cabinet above my desk. I used this in my research on Earth."

"I beg your pardon, Ma'am?" came the startled response of the tech specialist.

"You heard me correctly, MaryAnn. I plan to directly stimulate his neural-muscular junction and the CNS interface after priming him with the thallium."

Tapp saw the persistent questioning look on Sams face. Tapp explained, "I know this is highly experimental MaryAnn, but we've got to try something or he's going to die. We can't sustain him much longer and we all know this. I take full responsibility for the consequences. Now go get the stimulator and the thallium.

Now Lu, as she's getting the stimulator and the thallium, put these electrodes here over his temples, and here at the base of his skull, and those on his buttocks," said Tapp, pointing with her fingers to show the precise orientation she wanted. "When the stimulator is in place and connected to these electrodes it will create an artificial graviton field throughout Steve's nervous system."

Tapp continued to defend her unusual therapy with her nurse. "I know this is highly irregular Lu, but I'm out of options. The Commander is going to die unless we can stop and reverse the disintegration of his nervous system. Now get the stimulator attached and charge up the pulse generator to forty five joules."

Tapp was glad to see that Woolsey wasn't here to experience her desperation and witness her team's final battle. She wondered if Woolsey and the crew were following things through the video feed, but if they were there wasn't any communication. As the staff quickly moved to ready the treatment, Tapp could sense their relief at being given a task, even a hopeless one. She knew that everyone wanted heroic efforts, but there might soon come a time when futility would intervene and she would be forced to stop the resuscitation and let the Commander go. She had done this with patients before. It was always tough to lose anyone, but it would be tougher to lose a friend; and even tougher because they were all so far from home and so dependent on each other.

As her staff gave the thallium and they charged the neural stimulator, Tapp suddenly recalled a quote of Hippocrates, who once said, "Desperate illness sometimes requires desperate measures." She thought to herself, "I wonder if Hippocrates ever felt the weight of decision-making as much as I do now?"

CHAPTER 19

Because I could not stop for Death, He kindly stopped for me—the carriage held but just ourselves and immortality.

EMILY DICKINSON

Alpha Continent

Quixt's attention was suddenly diverted from the fascinating interaction between the Terrans and the People by the violent and nearly simultaneous deaths of two advanced minds half a world away. His advanced neural net registered the transcendence of those souls as one might feel a sudden breeze on the cheek. Quixt knew it was too late to save those minds, as he *saw* their essence fly through his sensors, past him toward eternity. Now all he could do was limit the damage. "How could I have been so preoccupied with Tenge and the Terrans that I ignored the second landing team? They must have encountered *Others*. What a disaster!" he sighed.

Quixt remained hidden by his inter-dimensional cloak and hovered between Tenge and Havel. His mind raced to understand his lack of awareness of the situation on the Beta continent. Perhaps the inter-dimensional cloak had obscured his sensory array in some unusual way. He had always trusted his sensory apparatus, which until now, missed little in the entire solar system. He thought, "Perhaps it wasn't my sensory array, but my distraction. All I know for sure is that I'm responsible for this tragedy. I should have at least considered that the Beta Team would encounter *Others*. Maybe I've underestimated them, these…hunters. Or maybe I've just been incredibly clumsy," he concluded with disgust.

He quickly shifted inter-dimensionally to the Beta continent, arriving in time to find the Terrans called Cooper and Snyder at the battle site. A quick assessment of the stricken Terran and the *Other* called !Kerrt confirmed that even he could do nothing to restore them. Quixt *visualized* their brains as darkly degenerating pulps of wreckage. He felt an intense sense of loss along with the guilt. His only comfort was his belief that all sentient creatures experienced transcendence to the Progenitor's realm.

"Small consolation for your screw up," he thought ruefully to himself. *Forgive me, Master,* he prayed. *I know these creatures suffered because of me. I pray that Grace will be sufficient even for me.*

Again, Quixt didn't expect a response, but often he experienced a sense of peace when he earnestly and humbly asked for forgiveness. "Now, get back to work," he told himself. It was his responsibility to get the situation under control.

Quixt scanned the mind of the *Other*, called !Zsakk, retreating in the distance. Quixt could see the confusion in the creature's mind. But there was something else, something unusual, as he probed. "!Zsakk mourns the loss of his…partner! What a strange concept for an *Other*," Quixt marveled. "I've never known this species to cooperate, let alone consider a partnership." Quixt could read the terror in !Zsakk's mind. "What a shock to learn that there are creatures more powerful than you," Quixt thought. But at the same time he felt compassion for the panther. "The creature has apparently been changed by its association with the female *Other*, and by her loss."

But there was something else in the hunter's mind. And suddenly Quixt recognized in the engrams of !Zsakk's mind the memories of !Kerrt. !Zsakk had absorbed !Kerrt! To Quixt's knowledge this had never happened before. And even more astounding was the revelation that !Zsakk had been in the process of establishing an interface to absorb the Terran named Hinton when he was driven off by Cooper and Snyder. "What a mess," Quixt sighed to himself. "What a mess."

Fortunately for Hinton the absorption process had not been very far along or Hinton would have been lost as well. In the process however, !Zsakk had gained considerable knowledge of the Terrans.

This expanded knowledge of the universe, coupled with the loss of !Kerrt, was perhaps too much for !Zsakk who was on the verge of a nervous breakdown. Quixt reached out with his mind and overlaid a sub-cortical calming engram in !Zsakk's mind, hoping that this subroutine would stabilize his sense of panic and disorientation.

Quixt next turned his attention to the one called Hinton, who was seriously injured by the stun pulse and the aborted neural interface with the *Other*. Quixt aggressively moved through Hinton's mind to shore up collapsing synapses and the complex neural algorithms that made a life form self-aware and alive.

As Quixt worked feverishly to save Hinton, he came upon memories in the Terran's mind. "What is man that you are mindful of him?" Quixt realized that the fragment came from the Terran Bible. Another notion came from an old hymn that went, "I wonder as I wander out under the sky..." This seemed especially poignant as Quixt tried to save the life of an entity with such a sublimely questioning mind.

He did all he dared to stabilize the human's injured mind. Quixt knew all too well that doing too much might aid survival, but result in insanity. He worked frantically during the long trip back to the Terran's landing craft. His goal was to keep Hinton alive till his crewmates could get him back to the ship.

Quixt was counting on Hinton's coma to mask his own presence as he raced through Hinton's mind. But there was no alternative; either take the risk of detection or allow Hinton to die. The damage was at the synaptic junctions of neurons throughout Hinton's nervous system. Quixt wondered whether the Terrans had the understanding or the technology to repair this type of damage.

Quixt's concerns were well founded when back on the Terran ship he queried their ship's computer and saw that the Terran's medical expertise would not be enough to save Hinton. Synaptic repair and dendritic brain manipulation were unfortunately beyond current Terran technology. Quixt continued to shore up collapsing neural interfaces, but how long could he keep this up? Quixt also worried that Terrans scanning devices might be able to detect him as he worked. And if Hinton survived would he become aware of Quixt as he regained consciousness? "I'll just have to risk it all," he concluded. "It's my mess to clean up."

As he worked on Hinton, Quixt remained hidden from the Terrans by staying in a higher dimensional configuration. His cloaking technique was effective, but would it impair his ability to keep tabs on the Alpha team? He'd already made this mistake once and dreaded the thought of another calamity. He gained some reassurance by monitoring data uplinks from the Alpha team through their com-link. For the time being he thought he could follow things well enough by using the Terran's technology that he was easily able to access and monitor.

The medical team quickly improved on the emergency treatment rendered by the landing team. Quixt managed to dodge most of their scanning beams. It was then that something of a miracle occurred. By gently probing the Terran's minds, Quixt found a potential solution to Hinton's injuries in Dr. Tapp's research experience. All Quixt had to do was gently loosen her reluctance to apply her research findings to Hinton's urgent problem. Once done, Quixt felt that the combination of neuro transmitter infusion, together with thallium infusion and stimulation by the graviton field, might actually stabilize further neuro-cortical cascade and reverse the damage. Gleefully, Quixt saw that Hinton could be saved! And he might even remember his interface with the *Other*. Would Hinton realize that the *Others* were sentient? Would the experience and the treatments even augment Hinton's neural function as suggested in Tapp's research? Quixt allowed himself the luxury of a brief sigh. "Perhaps this disaster can be salvaged. But can I get the doctor to take the chance?"

As he worked to influence Dr. Tapp, Quixt asked the void: *Perhaps this is your plan for humanity all along. Oh, I wish I could be sure of your Design, and my part, Lord! I wish you would just tell me what I should do. Don't you realize that we sometimes long for less choice and more direction?*

CHAPTER 20

I yam what I yam.
POPEYE, THE SAILOR MAN

A nightmarish collage of colors, shapes, sounds and smells floated through Hinton's mind; or was he a part of some bad dream? He concentrated on a bright light that seemed to move back and forth in front of him. It seemed more real than the roiling kaleidoscope of impressions all around him. He imagined himself falling from some high perspective back toward a place where he suddenly realized that the bright light was attached to the arm of Dr. Tapp who now hovered above him.

"He's waking up, Dr. Tapp!" cried Nurse Farmer. Everyone pushed forward with excitement and a renewed hope that had not been there just minutes before.

Tapp allowed the staff to press forward in their excitement. She murmured a bit self consciously and now with relief, "I guess everyone in the ship was watching us all along."

She recovered her composure and said, "I can see that, Lu", though Tapp was barely able to hide her joy behind her professional face. "Ms. Sams, please give me the readouts on the last Spec-MRI scan. And the rest of you, back up," she growled as crew members again threatened her ER from the hallway.

Tapp looked around and caught the eye of Ensign Dean Silber skulking at the doorway. "Mr. Silber, I guess Lieutenant Woolsey left you to keep an eye on us." She saw him squirm under her gaze, as if being caught stealing apples. "You seem to be the ranking officer of that rabble in the hall, so I want you to get everyone out of the Med Suite and then you can come back and be Woolsey's liaison. My patient is not out of the woods yet. If necessary, I'll clear the entire deck myself and you along with them!

"Yes, Ma'am!" snapped the ensign, glad that she hadn't lumped him with the "rabble." He quickly pushed everyone out of Tapp's ER and back into the hall, before returning to stand guard at the doorway. This afforded him a great view of the action. It was a lot better than the video monitors in the hallway.

Tapp was ecstatic, despite her gruffness brought on by the pressure and fatigue. Hinton's response had been dramatic and beyond her wildest expectations. She looked at the data and could see unequivocal improvement that matched the Commander's clinical response. She watched him as he struggled to regain his focus, and as he began moving all of his extremities purposefully for the first time. She had followed her instincts; she had given the proverbial wild ass guess "WAG" therapy and it was working! There was just no other explanation for the dramatic improvement in such a short time. "What a research paper," she dared to think. "That is if and when we ever get home."

"Mr. Hinton, can you hear me?" Tapp spoke loudly into Hinton's ear.

Hinton moved his head weakly toward the voice and managed a soft and coarse, "Yeah." It was all he could muster at the moment. The bright light moved again in front of his face, but he couldn't put it all together. He wondered briefly if he were having some kind of near-death experience. He was vaguely aware of other people moving around him as he fought to clear his mind. He continued to hear Dr. Tapp's voice and he thought to himself, "I must be back on the ship and in the med suite. How the hell could that be?" he wondered to himself. He struggled to look around. He tried to raise himself up and...

"Lie down, Sir!"

Hinton recognized the usually compassionate voice of the head nurse, Ms. Farmer. She sounded like she meant business and, under the circumstances, he was in no position to argue. He managed to quip, "Is that Nurse Ratchet, I'm hearing?"

Her serious face came into view above him and said, "Welcome back, Commander. But I'm not joking, Sir. You are not to sit up. You're back on the ship. You've been injured and you need to lie still and help us to help you."

"You'd better listen to her, Commander," interjected Tapp. "I've known her to tie unruly patients down," she joked, taking Hinton's hand in a soothing and reassuring way.

Actually Hinton was happy to lie still. He found that any movement made the room spin, as if he had way too much to drink. And he had felt very faint when he tried to sit up.

"What happened to me?" he thought. The last thing he remembered was walking in the forest with the Beta Team and "now I wake up back on the ship in the Med Suite under a doctor's care." As he searched his memory there were even stranger recollections, even one where he saw himself being shot by some type of energy weapon! He saw himself collapse as though he were watching the scene in a movie. And then it came to him: he was seeing through someone else's perspective! He somehow knew that the memory was valid, but it was not *his* memory. "How can that be?" he wondered to himself. "It's as though *my memory* and this other vision are both mine." And then a wash of the odd perceptions and strange sensations flooded his mind again, like the kaleidoscopic perceptions that he experienced on first awakening in the Med Suit. He could see his away team moving through the forest. He focused on the mental picture that was so real, so vivid. And the recollection abounded with colors and smells and sensations that he recognized, but he knew these were formerly unknown to him. For want of a better term, he described these perceptions as *Other*. There were also perspectives of what he knew to be animals in the forest. And there were startling smells that were so intense and so... alien. He now remembered a huge creature near him after the attack and Hinton then saw himself lying on the ground looking up at... the creature!

Hinton shook himself and opened his eyes to the reality of the ship and Dr. Tapp. "It's good to see you, Doc," he managed. "And I guess I'm glad to be here, but I'd rather not be looking up at you."

"That's understandable, Commander. You and the Beta Team were attacked and, as Lu mentioned, you were injured. You gave us quite a scare, but I believe you'll be all right now. We'll give you more details later. Are you in any pain? Can you remember anything about the attack?"

"Well, I've got a terrible headache and I'm really tired," said Hinton. "And I've got the strangest dreams or perceptions or whatever they are. It's as though I have memories that aren't mine. What kind of psychedelic shit, err medicine, are you giving me, Doc?"

Tapp smiled. "Commander, we didn't give you any psychotropic street drug. You actually got the best legal *designer* drugs I could muster." But Tapp was wondering herself, what were the side effects of the neural stimulators, neurotropin, and neurotransmitters, combined with the effects of apparent electrocution, shock, and resuscitation?

Hinton said "Is the Team safe?"

Tapp decided not to tell him about Grieve, but asked, "Do you feel up to talking about what you remember, Commander? I'd like your perspectives before the impressions fade."

"Yeah, I'm okay. Actually, I'm feeling steadily better." Hinton managed to turn himself up on his side and prop himself up on one arm. "But I don't think these memories will ever fade, Helen. It's like a lingering and vivid nightmare. Most dreams fade rapidly, but this one isn't fading at all. I remember lots of details about the attack and, I know this sounds crazy, but there are other memories that are just so intense and weird! And these other memories are different from any dream I've ever had. It's as though I'm living in the forest on the planet and experiencing the sounds and smells and even the visual perspectives of *another* creature! The smells are the real cincher; there's no way I could imagine the things I smell. And there are just no words that I can find to describe these sensations to you. What's happened to me, Doc? Am I losing my mind?"

"No, Commander, you're not losing your mind," said Tapp. "I don't really have an explanation for these unusual memories you have or the visions, as you call them. We used a lot of medications on you and perhaps these, along with your injuries, caused the memory anomalies."

"Well, I want you to know they're pretty terrifying," replied Hinton. "The bizarre recollections just keep coming as I concentrate on the attack."

Tapp observed that Hinton was getting increasingly excited and agitated. His voice was becoming higher and his eyes began darting back and forth. He said, "I can see heavy sheets of rain caught as in the strobe-light effects of lightening. I can remember seeing purple, insect-like creatures, as big as my thumb, buzzing around each other in a mating dance in mid air. And I see my team coming through the forest, but from the perspective of someone else! It's like seeing a movie, but in real time and with all the impressions of touch, smell, and...more."

Hinton suddenly turned toward Tapp with a sense of horror written across his face. "I'm seeing the world from the perspective of one of the creatures who attacked us! His memories are in my mind, Doc. He calls himself ...!Zsakk."

CHAPTER 21

For what I do is me.
ANNIE DILLARD

Alpha Continent

Why must you go back to see these…foreigners, as you call them? asked Kitu plaintively.

Wife of mine, we've been over this and over this. This is important to our People and it is important to me, explained Tenge, hoping she did not detect his frustration with her unwillingness to see his perspective.

Well, why can't someone else go to meet the strangers? she pleaded, almost without waiting for his thought to be completed. *Why can't the Elders go alone?*

I gave my word to their Captain Havel that I would come back and bring the Elders of the Village. My word is my bond and you know that. Besides, this is what I've imagined all my life. I have to go, Kitu. I need to do this!

This whole story is just too unbelievable! Kitu said shaking her head anxiously as she watched Tenge preparing his day pack. *Husband of mine, don't you understand that I'm afraid for you and for us all?*

He stopped his packing and turned to face her. She was visibly trembling and he took her in his arms. *Yes, Kitu,* he consoled. *I know you are afraid. And, to a certain extent, I am afraid also. But this is something that I must do. The arrival of these travelers is…important for*

141

us all. I know that you don't see things as I do, but I am asking you to trust me and to trust my judgment.

Well, what did the Elders say when you told them of the foreigners and asked for a Council meeting?

*The Elders were skeptical, but they agreed to a Council meeting because I showed them the Travelers' talking machine. They couldn't discount my story then because they couldn't ignore this talking box. Kitu, you know me better than they do. You must know that I am telling the truth. Something wonderful has happened! We are not **alone**!*

Well, of course we are not alone, replied Kitu. *We live in the Village and on the World. We have friends and a life together and you are risking it all—and for what? I don't see any benefit for the Village or our family through contact with these intruders.*

Tenge could see her genuine fear and sensed the exasperation in his wife's thoughts. He could partly understand her reaction. How could he expect anyone to appreciate this passion of his? He tried to reassure himself thinking, "I can't just lie to myself nor can I ignore the fact that the Terrans are here." Even though they said that they would honor the wishes of the Village and leave if asked to do so, Tenge felt they would just try and make contact with another Village.

Kitu, my love, please look into my thoughts and try to see the wonder of this incident. Yes, we have each other, our lives, and the World, but these foreigners are proof that there are other worlds and other creatures, just as I have imagined all my life! My dreams are not fantasies; they are a reality. Look into my mind and try to glimpse the possibilities for us and the rest of the Village.

He felt her mind flutter over his, and then her body softened in his arms. She projected: *Yes, I can see what this means to you, husband of mine. But I want you to look into my heart. This scares me for reasons beyond the security of our family and our Village. If these beings are what you say, I'm so afraid that you will follow your dream and leave me and Roosa. I'm afraid that we will be replaced by your dreams, Tenge.*

His heart melted as he finally understood his wife's real concern. "How could I have been so stupid?" he wondered inwardly. He felt guilty to be so consumed by his own passion, that he didn't see the challenge to his soul-mate. The meeting with the Terrans and the meeting with the Elders had caused him to overlook Kitu's real concern.

He gently inclined his head forward to touch hers in their *bonding embrace*. He slowly recited the mantric ritual that removed all barriers between his mind and his beloved. *Kitu, my mind and heart are open to you*, he intoned over and over. He felt her respond to him and saw her mind recite the corresponding bonding mantra.

They found themselves floating in their special place, as much imagined as real, where only lovers can go; a place of trust and openness that transcends the individual. A "mountaintop" experience shared with another and with such intensity that it would consume them both if sustained for too long. The rush of passion was brief, yet intense, quickly morphing into the after glow of oneness as only the merging of two souls can experience.

He thought softly: *I love you, Kitu, with all my being. Nothing can change that. I could never turn my back on you and Roosa. But I must go and meet these travelers. Ignoring them will not make them go away or allow us to live as we did before yesterday. We can't go back to a time before*, consoled Tenge.

Kitu floated beside him in their embrace but persisted only gently now. *Who is going with you to see these creatures? You must take the Elders. Will they convene a war council?*

No, there will be no War Council. These travelers are very powerful. It would be foolish and useless for us to behave aggressively, Kitu. If they are powerful enough to come from another star, from one of the blinking lights in the sky that I am always pointing out to you, it would be foolish to attack them. And I am convinced that the Terrans are not dangerous. I have looked into their thoughts. I am convinced that they are peaceful.

What is this you say, another star? she gently teased him. *Stories of the lights in the sky are tales for children told around the fire by foolish old men!*

Well, I am not an old man, he countered playfully as he figuratively winked at her.

No, I can vouch for that! she blushed.

Tenge considered: *But you're right Kitu. I don't have any direct proof of what the travelers say, but I have considered these lights all my life. I have told you many times that I believe the lights are those of far away suns, like our own sun that makes things grow and makes our lives possible. I have always sensed this truth, but now I have seen some confirmation of my dreams by the travelers. Do you not see how liberating this is for me? I saw into the mind of their Captain Havel, and I saw the truth about the stars! I saw through their eyes the visions of their home world so far away, Kitu. I never wanted to be different, but I am. And if you search my thoughts you will be able to see the thoughts of these Humans. Analyze their thoughts yourself.*

I love you, husband of mine. And, yes, I "see" the Human's thoughts. They are indeed strange. How do you know that you have not been tricked by these foreigners? Perhaps I should go with you and meet these Humans myself and see if their thoughts are true.

Mother of mine, you do not need to worry about Father, and you do not need to go to the Humans. I will go with Father and meet them.

The thoughts of their daughter Roosa burst in upon their private reverie and literally jerked them back to reality. They were stunned to feel the powerful force of their daughter's mind. They momentarily felt awkward in the universal shock of all parents caught in a moment of intimacy by their children. Walking forward into their sleep-room, Roosa sensed their confusion and embarrassment, so she halted out of respect, and then reached gently into their minds to calm their thoughts of self consciousness.

Parents of mine, I know that you are shocked by my intrusion and I am sorry for invading your privacy. Also, I sense your surprise by the power of my mind. To a great extent I have concealed myself from you all these cycles. For this deception I ask your forgiveness. My plan was to gradually make you more aware of my visions and my destiny, but the arrival of the Humans has forced an acceleration of my schedule. Don't be afraid; something wonderful is about to happen!

CHAPTER 22

The sun shines not on us, but in us.
JOHN MUIR

Alpha Continent

Havel wrestled with the decision to stay on the planet and await the return of Tenge and the People. Was he being stupid and letting his passion override sound judgment? He had to admit that Lieutenant Woolsey's logic was sound. There was little he could do to help his friend, Commander Hinton or ease the loss of Private Grieve. Now with the Beta team back on the ship, Havel convinced himself that the opportunity of contact exceeded the risks.

Woolsey's report that Hinton was improving assured Havel that he was doing the right thing. Woolsey had also sent a second team to the Beta continent and his marines had recovered the body of Private Grieve. Xenobiology assistant Brown McCormick had accompanied the marines and had completed a detailed scanning of the alien "panther" that had attacked the Beta team. He brought back a treasure trove of data that would hopefully solve the mystery of its weapon system.

"Very good work, Lieutenant," said Havel. It's probably just as well that I'm here and not on the ship. I might not have authorized a second trip to the Beta continent at this time."

"Thank you, Sir. I know there was some risk, but I felt the rescue party would be relatively safe. Our detailed scans of the area

145

showed none of the panthers close by. We know what to look for now, Captain. I don't think they'll surprise us again. I'm sorry for burning the additional reaction mass with the second landing, but I thought we needed the data and I thought it would be good for morale to bring Mr. Grieve back to the ship. I'll make the next scheduled report to you at 0600 hours, and I'll call you sooner if there is any change in Mr. Hinton."

"Thank you, Lieutenant. I've decided to stay on the planet overnight, in part to make up for the expense of the reaction mass from the second trip to Beta, but also because I believe we're safe within the energy screen. I expect Tenge here early tomorrow, and I doubt we could conceal another landing in this area."

"I understand, Captain. We'll continue to monitor your area carefully for hostiles, but we've seen none of the energy signatures like those on the southern continent use. Woolsey out."

Havel returned his concentration to the Alpha team's situation. He thought things were under as good a control as he could organize. The energy field around the landing craft extended thirty meters. After news of the attack on the Beta team there were no complaints from anyone when he ordered them to remain within the energy field's perimeter at all times. Havel smiled to see that the scientist's now found plenty to study within the thirty meters of the boat and no longer whined about his restrictions.

Several crewmembers decided to sleep within the cramped cabin of the landing craft during the night, but Havel decided to put his cot and sleeping bag outside with the marines who were rotating on sentry duty. Looking up at the strange star patterns, he realized that he had never been outside on an alien planet at night. He had landed on several planets within the Sol system and several other planets during *Odyssey's* travels, but he had always slept in a protected enclosure or returned to an orbiting ship. He thought about how different his perspective was lying on his back looking up at twinkling stars that had no familiar pattern. The night was dark and the sky was awash with countless stars. Looking toward the horizon he saw this world's two small moons just rising. They reflected minimal light and only added to the strangeness of the night sky above him.

Havel lay there listening to the myriad nighttime noises from the nearby forest. He thought, "I guess the ancient struggle between hunters and the hunted exists here like everywhere else." He woke up several times during the night to those shrieks from the forest, but was reassured by the marines that their scans revealed nothing larger than the passing of something the size of a large dog. Two other times a creature of the night brushed their energy screen and was sent scurrying with a yowl and the smell of ozone and burnt flesh.

The night passed uneventfully and morning found them reasonably rested and ready for the expected meeting with the People. The report from *Odyssey* was good. Mr. Hinton remained stable and was apparently recovering rapidly. And the analysis of the alien panther-like creature revealed important data that would enable them to understand the alien weapon.

"Captain, it appears that Mr. Grieve died by electrocution," said Mr. Woolsey. "The 'panther' possesses what appears to be a natural bio-capacitor in its chest and has the ability to produce electricity, store a huge charge and then discharge a focused energy pulse of electricity much like a lightening bolt. Fortunately for Sergeant Cooper and Dr. Snyder, it takes the creature some time to recharge and fire again. Dr. Tapp also wanted you to know that Commander Hinton seems to have experienced some type of neural linkage with the alien. It seems that after he was paralyzed by the energy pulse, the creature may have been trying to feed on the Commander when Cooper drove it off."

"That's incredible, John. What do you mean by a neural linkage with the alien, Lieutenant?"

"I really don't know anything for sure, Sir. Dr. Tapp was really busy with the Commander. She threw me out of the med suite early on and has ejected everyone else now. She's stationed a guard at the door! But he's my man and I get regular reports from him. Her preliminary report alleges that something happened to Hinton beyond his being hit by an energy weapon. He vividly recalls his attacker and the Doc says he has shared memories of the alien. These include sounds and smells and sensations otherwise completely foreign to Commander Hinton. According to Dr. Tapp, Hinton is recalling more and more as he recovers and that a merging of minds may be part of the creature's feeding process. Hinton is convinced that the creature is intelligent and was hunting them as a source of food!"

Havel interrupted Woolsey's report with another, "That's astounding!"

"Yes, Sir, it is," intoned Woolsey, who was determined to appear dispassionate and act as a Captain should. "We have continued to scan your area, in particular, and the rest of the Alpha continent, but we haven't seen any energy discharges as we see regularly on the Beta continent. We have even been able to see what we think are other panthers on Beta with infra red scanning. There is nothing similar on the Alpha continent."

"Lieutenant, do you realize how astonishing this is? We've been to dozens of star systems and now we come upon a planet with two sentient life forms that are vastly different. Have we detected any signs of technology on the Beta continent?"

"No, Sir. We've carefully reviewed all our scans and the data Dr. Nixon collected. He thinks the anomalous readings we were getting as we approached the planet were from the alien's energy beams. We've found no organized constructions or other energy signatures on Beta, aside from considerable seismic activity. By scanning we have detected other large life forms on the Beta continent. These appear to be groups of large quadrupeds whose tracks Hinton's team found. Perhaps these are the principal prey of the panthers."

"Good report, Mr. Woolsey. I am reassured that there are no panthers near us," said Havel. "Perhaps these land masses are so far removed that the life forms evolved totally separate of each other; possibly like the evolution of life on the Australian continent. I'll run this theory by Dr. Wade in a few minutes."

Havel continued, "This does raise an added security issue though. Suppose the People possess this energy weapon in addition to their apparent telepathic ability. This could pose a real risk to the team."

Woolsey countered, "Sir, we've been scanning the Alpha continent continuously and we've seen no energy signatures as we see routinely on Beta. The energy discharges are easy to spot, now that we know what to look for. I can't imagine an entire continent without any energy discharges over time, so I suspect the People don't possess this type of weapon."

"Your logic is quite sound, Mr. Woolsey. And I'm reasonably assured of our superior firepower, especially now that we are aware of the potential danger. We've seen no evidence of the hostility that Hinton's team encountered, nor did I sense any from the alien, Tenge. We'll just have to stay sharp and keep the risks as low as possible."

"We're all excited, Captain, and we'll be watching closely. Would you like me to send down the other boat and more marines?"

"No, I don't think that would be wise; it might alarm the aliens," said Havel. Thinking out loud he said, "Perhaps I could extend the energy field out from the boat a greater distance and have the aliens meet us across the energy perimeter. But again, I'm afraid all of this will damage trust. I sensed no deception in Tenge's mind yesterday. He certainly could be setting us up, but I just don't believe it."

"Sir, how do you know that you're reading his intentions correctly? I'm not questioning your decision, but it's my responsibility to point out alternatives," said Woolsey.

"No offense taken, Lieutenant. I appreciate your concerns. You're right, I can't be sure that I'm reading his thoughts correctly, nor can I be sure he understands me, for that matter. This meeting is just too important to try and overanalyze and put additional safeguards in place that might needlessly jeopardize contact and relationship. I'm just going to have to trust my gut feelings on this one, John. I just hope that the others in Tenge's village come with a mind as open as his seems to be."

CHAPTER 23

Reality is always more than what we see.
EDMUND BURKE

Alpha Continent

Tenge struggled with his composure as he stood before his child who was obviously much more than he or Kitu had ever imagined. It was unheard of for one so young to possess such clarity of thought, such control of her mind, or such obvious maturity. Furthermore, Tenge sensed a vast intellect, as his daughter touched his mind. He recognized a calming algorithm that his precocious daughter was using to allay their fears. This was in itself disturbing; there was a taboo among the People for mind and emotional manipulation.

He and Kitu had always been aware that Roosa was special, but this was something much more, of that he was sure. He caught himself being momentarily fearful of his own daughter and the strangeness of the situation. He asked himself, "Is she a monster?" He shuddered to even think such a thing. This was his beloved Roosa standing before him; but she seemed to be even more than an adult.

No, Father of mine, I am not a monster. Forgive me for my use of a calming algorithm. Look into my thoughts and see that my actions are virtuous. I didn't want things to occur so suddenly for you; I was just trying to ease the adjustment pain and your anxiety. I will stop all thoughts other than those necessary for us to communicate and understand each other.

Again the clarity in her thoughts was striking to Tenge. He thought to himself, "There is no confusion in her thoughts; there is no sign of a child's manipulation of the truth. And again, there are the glimpses of an intellect that seems limitless. Where did she get these thoughts? And how has she been able to hide her true nature from Kitu and me?"

Tenge looked around to see Kitu sitting slumped on the side of the bed with her face in her hands, sobbing softly. His own knees felt weak and he looked for a chair to sit down for fear he might faint. As he sat down beside Kitu he put his arm around her shoulders to try and console her. Roosa approached them.

Father of mine, I am so sorry to upset you and mother. I know this is such a shock for you both to realize the depth of my thoughts. I did not want things to be this way. I really did not think it was my time; this is why I have not been completely open with you. It has only now been revealed to me by our Maker that it is my time.

Tenge reeled with each brush of Roosa's powerful mind. His poor wife was in shock and he saw horror in her thoughts. He wondered, "Will Kitu reject Roosa? Can she accept the revelation that Roosa is not a child? And what will the Villagers do if they learn the truth about Roosa? How will I be able to protect her?"

Roosa, I'm very confused and more than a little scared; mostly, I'm concerned about you. I...

Tenge's thoughts were interrupted by a scream from Kitu's mind. *What are you? What will happen to us? You can't let anyone know of this! The Village will say you are evil. They will destroy you or drive you away. Oh, Tenge, what will happen to her, to us, to our family?*

Mother of mine, please hear me and trust me; everything will be fine, soothed Roosa. *Perhaps I should have prepared you and Father, but I thought there would be more time. In some ways the arrival of the Humans is as much a surprise for me as it is for you. I have always known that I have a special purpose, but I never knew what it would be. I can now see the path that I must take, that we all must take.*

Tenge broke in saying: *Roosa, what do you mean our Maker told you it is your time? Are you saying that you speak with... God?*

The arrival of the travelers is a sign for me, Father of mine. I must go to the Council with you and discuss the situation with the Elders. It is my destiny to meet the Humans. I know this will cause much controversy in the Village and stress on our family. Some in the Village will fear me; others will believe in me. But the Maker, the Father of everything that is, will protect us. He has shown me the Way. He has set up these conditions to announce my time. I open my mind to you both. Look there for the Truth!

Kitu's mind raced as her entire world spun dizzily around her. She said to herself, "What am I supposed to do? This is my child, but she is suddenly no longer a child! She will become an outcast and our family will be despised."

Kitu thought: *Roosa, my child, my life, I fear for you! This seems so foolish to think of you now as my little one; yet you were my child ten minutes ago! So what are you now? What have you become?*

I have not become anything, Mother of mine. I have just made you aware of my destiny. What am I? I am a child of the One. I am The Child of the One. I am the fulfillment of prophesy. I am the embodiment of the Maker!

Tenge felt as though he was seeing the three of them from somewhere outside his own body. He imagined himself looking at a play and trying to figure out what would come next. His daughter had just revealed that she was no longer a child and that God himself had a plan for her! And this was not a metaphorical plan, but a specific one. She proclaims herself as the anointed one! He studied Roosa's mind and he knew she was rational, despite her mind-boggling story. Roosa was speaking what she knew to be the truth. Tenge thought it might have been easier if she were irrational, even crazy. At least she would still be their Roosa, and she would still need them. At least something of the past would not change.

Tenge's mind raced as he contemplated the seemingly impossible. He especially worried about Kitu. Tenge knew that her belief system was very rigid and was the foundation of her being. Would Roosa's shocking revelation cause her to snap and push her into a breakdown? Their child stood there before them stating that she was the One whom prophecy said would come to lead the People. The focus of Kitu's entire belief system was standing in their sleep-room! He wondered to himself whether this was an epiphany or something else. Roosa's revelation would have been easier if this was someone else's story, and Tenge had just heard it in the temple!

Roosa moved closer to them and stretched out her arms encircling their shoulders. *Come, Father and Mother of mine. The Kingdom is at hand! And it will be made known to all who can see.*

CHAPTER 24

God exists out of time and place.
C. S. LEWIS

Quixt was ecstatic with the medical team's results. All Tapp needed was just a gentle nudge, a subtle encouragement to follow her instincts and the insights from her research. Quixt waxed philosophical, "Sometimes it takes so little to change a life." Hinton was going to make it and he would be able to remove himself from his support role. "It's just as well," he sighed. "I've done enough for one day," as he berated himself for the tragedies that occurred on his watch.

Quixt scanned Hinton as he recovered. The memories of the attack were there and were surfacing. But Quixt could also see the changes in Hinton's mind resulting from his bonding with !Zsakk. "Those changes will be permanent," he sighed to himself. "But maybe some good can come out of this." He could see enhancements written in engrams across Hinton's neocortex. Had the bonding process with the *Other* and the medical therapy caused the millions of new dendritic connections in Hinton's brain? Quixt would have predicted that the *Other's* thought patterns would fade as soon as the "absorption" process was interrupted. But maybe the doctor's drug concoctions and medical treatments during Hinton's resuscitation effected the permanent enhancements in Hinton's brain. Quixt suddenly realized that with these enhancements Hinton might now be capable of a new level of function, perhaps even telepathy like the *Others* and the People! Perhaps this disaster had opened up a new opportunity for the Terrans. Quixt directed his thoughts outward again: *Is this all part of your Design?*

Whatever the results, it was obvious to Quixt that he was no longer needed on the Terran's ship. "It's time to check on the Village before their meeting with the Terrans, Mr. Quixt."

Shifting inter-dimensionally to the planet and to the People's Village, Quixt immediately noted a change in the minds of the Villagers. "They are afraid," he realized with a degree of amazement. He had not seen fear in them for a very long time. In fact, their perpetual calmness was a sign of their problem. It was their complacency and perhaps their connection to each other and their surroundings that had resulted in stagnation. His efforts to gently push them forward had been difficult and not very rewarding to date.

And to Quixt's amazement, a child was telepathically speaking before the Elder's council and the Village! Quixt did not know the child, but she must be quite precocious. But there was something else about this child as he probed and analyzed her mind. He was shocked to confront an intellect that was so vast it made him recoil in surprise. He cried out in shock: *It is you, my Lord!*

The God-child answered his revelation with a soft, but forceful: *Be silent, my Quixt. You are to only observe until I ask you to do otherwise.*

He managed a weak: *Yes, my Lord.* He doubted he could do otherwise from the shock of seeing the Progenitor here in the Village embodied in this child.

Turning from the mind of the cloaked Quixt, Roosa continued with the Villagers: *People of our Village, hear me! I am not a monster as some of you are wondering. Nor am I possessed of evil as others are thinking. Look into my mind and see the truth of what I say. You know that we cannot lie to each other when the defenses of our minds are removed. I open myself to you. Now open your eyes and hearts to prophesy. It is said that the Maker will bring the One. You have seen prophesy fulfilled today. If I were evil, you and the Elders could see this with my mind open to you. I come before you to announce that I am the One!*

Standing beside his daughter, Tenge literally heard and felt a collective gasp in the minds of the Villagers.

Blasphemer! came the shrill cry from someone's mind in the crowd.

Another thought: *How can she be the One? Is this not the child of Tenge and Kitu?*

Another mind shouted: *You are wrong! This child's thoughts are clear and virtuous. I sense in her the truth!*

Silence, all of you! said Rotan, the Chief Elder, with an icy blast of his mind. *We are here to listen to Tenge and to discuss how we should deal with the foreigners. Roosa is a child. She is not of age, and is not entitled to address this Council.*

Let her speak, Rotan! challenged someone in the crowd.

Tenge was grateful for even the limited support he felt, but he could also feel the hostility and the fear in the minds of many more. And then suddenly, as if cool water had been poured over him, his apprehension abated. He felt strangely at peace with what should have been a frightening situation. And then he saw clearly what he must do and what he should say.

Friends, please hear me! I asked for this meeting to tell you about the foreigners that have come. These strangers are from far away and want to meet us. I believe it is very important for us to welcome them. They are very different from us, but their minds are pure. They call themselves Humans and have come from farther away than even across the Great Water. We must not ignore them. Though they told me they would leave us alone if that is our choice, I fear they will then just go to another village and we will lose this great opportunity. I know that most of you laughed at my speculations of other places, but now these travelers offer proof. We cannot run from the truth. We must go and meet with them.

Tenge paused. He had their attention and apparently the Council was going to hear him out. Tenge continued quickly before he lost the advantage. *My friends and neighbors, all of you know me and my family, so I ask you to open your minds to what I am about to say. I thought the arrival of the humans was the most important thing that had ever happened for our People. But now this is dwarfed by what can only be described as "the epiphany" which is now occurring in our midst. My Roosa asked you to search her mind for the truth. We People are not creatures that can easily lie to each other. Kitu and I are more shocked than any of you by Roosa's words and the power of her mind. But I can see that*

157

she speaks the truth. And if you are honest with yourselves you know this to be true as well. She is the One prophesized in the sacred scriptures!

A silence fell over the gathering. Rotan recovered and then thundered with a sneer: *You will be silent, Tenge! And you...,* Rotan paused, raising his hand and pointing his finger at Roosa, *do not come into my mind or the People's mind again! What are you? How can a mere child touch the minds of all of us at once? What evil sorcery works in you?*

Roosa stood her ground and confidently replied to everyone: *I can speak to all of you at once and with the mind of an adult because "I am" the fulfillment of scripture. I have never used these powers and have always resisted these feelings until today. Yet I have always known that I was different than others. Search my mind and know me! I can no more lie to you than I can deny myself or my destiny.*

You are an Abomination! came a blast of condemnation from a villager.

Tenge turned to see Lamek, not ten meters away, covering his ears with his hands, as if this would stop the powerful mind that was speaking to them all.

Drive her and her kind away, shouted a Council member, as he shook a clenched fist at Roosa and took several steps toward her.

Tenge was worried that they might be in danger. But then Roosa declared with such force and power and with such confidence that no one dared move: *There will be no violence here today! Put these destructive thoughts out of your minds.* Tenge sensed the mood of the Village change suddenly and he knew that the moment of danger had passed. No one dared challenge the power of Roosa's mind!

Roosa then spoke with such power that Tenge saw the Council member sag to his knees. *My People! You cannot suppress this truth or ignore the arrival of the humans. Nor can you deny me. I am here before you asking you to open your minds to the truth. Did not the ancient writings say that the One would not be accepted in his Village?*

Rotan raised his hand for attention as he tried to reassert his leadership authority. He sneered confidently: *The scriptures say that the One will not be accepted in "his village." There is nothing about a woman, let alone a mere child, being the One.*

With Rotan's quote of scripture, Tenge again detected threatening thoughts directed toward Roosa. He worried that this was too much for the Village to handle and his normally calm friends might act with murderous intent.

Rotan, I know that you think you are protecting the People, soothed Roosa. *But you cannot silence me or change the destiny before us. I will speak to the People and I will go with my father to meet the humans.*

The power and the finality of Roosa's thoughts reverberated in the minds of everyone assembled. Tenge saw Rotan seem to falter under the weight and power of Roosa's declaration.

Roosa continued: *Whether my father and I go alone to meet the humans is your only decision.*

Quixt hovered, frozen by the astounding events before him. He was shocked that he had never suspected Roosa as being special. "How could I have missed this powerful mind?" he wondered. When the Villagers had threatening thoughts, he had concern for Tenge and Roosa and he briefly wondered if he would have to intervene to prevent the mob from attacking them. He scanned the minds of the Villagers looking for a way to diffuse the passion that he sensed was about to erupt. But to his great surprise he found Roosa's mind already there adjusting the anger and tension in the Villager's minds! The mind of the "child" was there actually looking back at him and smiling. *We are in no danger, Quixt. You do not need to intervene.* He was sure his knees would have buckled under him if he had been a corporeal being and had legs.

He addressed the mind in the body of the child. *My Lord, you are here!* he rejoiced. *Do you want me to shift into a three dimensional form so that I can proclaim your presence to these unbelievers?*

That isn't necessary, my Quixt. I don't believe the People need another shock. The arrival of the Terrans and my pronouncement are enough for them to process at this time. But you still don't recognize me, do you? You haven't grasped the full truth yet.

Almost wounded Quixt responded passionately: *Yes, my Lord! You are The Progenitor! You are the source of all that is! You are the One!*

Yes, my Quixt, that is true. But you search for me in your prayers to the void and you search for me here in the Village. You now look for me within Roosa. Understand this, my faithful servant. I have always existed and I am everywhere. I am the Progenitor. And I am here now as Roosa, as I was Jesus long ago on Earth! I have come to my children on numberless worlds throughout all of time. I have come to them with as many names as there are stars in the night sky.

CHAPTER 25

There is a God shaped vacuum in the heart of
every person.
BLAISE PASCAL

Alpha Continent

The small group of aliens emerged from the forest shortly after first light, making no move to advance further. Havel was prepared for the arrival this time. The alien's approach was easily detected through active scanning and everyone was positioned well before the aliens came through the tree line.

It was predetermined that Havel, Walker, and Wade would again go out to meet the aliens. They would have to leave the protection of the energy field, but it couldn't be helped. "So much was riding on this meeting," Havel thought. "The benefits surely justify the risks," he kept telling himself. Things had worked out before; he hoped they would again.

As the three humans walked slowly toward the aliens, Havel easily recognized Tenge. He thought about waving, but decided against that; the gesture might be considered provocative. He opened his mind as he had done the day before, but he detected nothing. Havel noticed that there was a smaller alien among the three larger ones. "Was this a juvenile?" he wondered. The three humans stopped about thirty meters from the four aliens and waited. In short order Havel noticed that the small alien turned its head ever so slightly toward the others and then the smaller alien and Tenge advanced forward toward them. When the two aliens started toward them, Havel signaled for the three humans to move forward again. They all stopped about ten meters from each other and waited. Nothing happened. Havel framed his words and focused his thoughts on Tenge, but again there was no response. Havel began to be concerned by the increasingly uncomfortable silence. Had he been wrong about communicating with Tenge yesterday? Were yesterday's impressions just wistful thinking?

"Bill, I'm going to step forward about half way to the aliens. You and Linda stay here and watch my backside."

"Are you sure this is wise, Captain? I mean, we're already very exposed and we accomplished so much yesterday at this same distance."

"I'm not getting anything from the aliens, Bill. I think we need to make the next move."

"It's your call, Captain. I agree with you that things do seem different today. I'm not sensing anything, whereas yesterday we all felt something."

Havel moved forward slowly and as he moved forward so did Tenge and the small alien. Walker observed them all stop about two meters from each other. He saw Havel raise his right hand slowly with his palm open as one would do when getting ready to give a wave.

Suddenly there was a blinding flash of light around the aliens and the Captain. Walker flinched instinctively and crouched as he drew his side arm. He scanned the area in all directions for the hostiles that he knew must already be on the attack. But he saw nothing except the boat, the two aliens at the forest's edge and Dr. Wade who stood there with a look of shock on her face. He turned his gaze back to the meeting area and the Captain. The two aliens and the Captain were now within what appeared to be an opalescent shimmering energy field. Walker called frantically to the Captain as he rushed to the edge of the field. There was no response. He could dimly see through the foggy wall of energy and saw the Captain lying on the grass beside the larger alien. The smaller alien just stood motionless beside the other two.

"The Captain has been attacked!" he frantically called over the com-link. "He and the two aliens are enclosed in what appears to be an energy field. The Captain is not responding to my calls and is down!"

"What do you want us to do, Doc?" came the urgent reply from Sergeant Parrott. "Are you and Dr. Wade okay?"

"Wade and I are fine. It's the Captain that I'm worried about. Are there any other hostiles in the area?"

"There's nothing out there except the two aliens at the forest edge, Sir, and they haven't moved. Do you want us to move forward to support you? Should we fire on the screen?" asked the Sergeant.

Walker tried to assess the Captain and the alien called Tenge. He reported, "The Captain seems to be breathing evenly and his eyes are closed as if he's asleep. The one called Tenge is also down and isn't moving either. It is breathing and its lower eyes are closed just like the Captain's. That creepy upper eye is just staring at nothing. Everyone, hold your position for now and don't fire; the laser cannon could injure the Captain. Are you getting any readings on the Captain, Ensign Grubb?"

"Yeah, we're getting a surprisingly clear signal and data stream. His telemetry does look like he's asleep."

Walker felt Wade approach his side and he saw her toss a small pebble against the shimmering boundary. It bounced off with a soft "boomp" like a pool ball hitting a rubbery cushion.

"Don't touch anything, Linda!"

"I don't plan to," she assured Walker without looking up. She continued to study the energy field with her field scanner.

"Bill, I believe the small alien is a female."

"How do you know that?" asked Walker.

"I don't know," said Wade, alternately looking at her scanner and the alien. "I just sense this. Call it woman's intuition. Are you getting communication like the Captain reported yesterday?"

Walker stopped and considered her question carefully, focusing on the probing eyes of the alien. "I don't know..." he paused and concentrated. "Maybe I do sense something, but nothing specific. What about you?"

"I'm getting some fleeting thoughts and images of things that I don't understand. Look at the Captain's eyelids, Bill! They're fluttering just like he's in REM sleep and dreaming."

Manning the boat's communication panel, Private Venable reported, "Dr. Walker, *Odyssey* is receiving real time data links from you.

They wanted me to report that they have been unable to determine the source of the energy field or its nature."

"Thanks, Jeff," said Wade. "Where is Private Foulk?"

"I'm here at the laser cannon, Doc. The Sarge told me to cover you while he moved to watch the other aliens. He's about forty meters to your right and has a plasma rifle covering the two aliens at the forest edge."

"Thanks, Steph. I hope we won't need your firepower. I'm afraid that Bill and I are a bit too close for the cannon. We don't even know if the laser could penetrate the shield; it might just reflect off of it and fry us as well," said Wade.

"Well if I do have to fire I'll shout, '*hit the deck, Doc!*'" said the marine, whose bravado certainly exuded more confidence than she had.

"Lieutenant Woolsey, are you there?"

"Yes, Dr. Walker, we're following everything you do. What is the young alien doing?"

"She's just standing there looking at us, John."

Woolsey said, "Does anyone down there sense anything?"

"Not much," said Wade, "just some vague impressions. Bill and I have tried to form words in our minds and then focus the thoughts at the aliens as the Captain described to us. But we've gotten no response. We haven't tried to interact with the other aliens at the forest's edge. Sergeant Parrott is covering them."

Woolsey continued, "Does it seem to you that the small alien is in control of things or is she being controlled?"

"That's really a good question, Lieutenant," said Wade. "The small alien just stands there looking at us. Her manner is certainly commanding or complicit with the events."

"Mr. Woolsey, what do you think about probing the field?" said Walker. "It seemed harmless when Linda tossed a pebble against it. I think we need to try and do something to get to the Captain."

Woolsey continued. "I agree we need to try something and we really don't have any other suggestions. Go ahead and try to force the situation."

Stepping forward Walker reached out and gingerly touched the screen's edge and immediately pulled his hand back as if he'd touched something hot on the stove. "It feels rubbery and there was a slight tingling sensation in my fingers and up my arm as I made contact." He touched the field again and this time pushed harder. Walker saw his hand indent the surface as he pushed. As he pushed the tingling increased and became increasingly uncomfortable. He reported, "As I push there is more resistance and a sensation of heat up my arm."

Apparently everyone was watching, because multiple scientists began speculating over the com-link prompting Woolsey to bark, "Everyone get off the com! We can't communicate with our people on the ground with everyone interrupting. If you have an observation, pipe it through to the bridge. Go ahead, Bill."

As Walker continued to push, the resistance and the hot tingling sensation continued until he could stand it no longer. He jumped back shaking his hand as if his entire arm had gone to sleep. "Lieutenant, we're not going to get through this shield easily."

CHAPTER 26

Beta Continent

In the two day-cycles since the death of !Kerrt, !Zsakk had wandered aimlessly through the forest. He was plagued by the intense, yet strange, sensation of loss. Never before had he been aware of this... *feeling*. Never before had he experienced a sense of sadness over the death of anything, let alone an *Other*. The creatures of !Zsakk's reality had always been either food or competition. The only exception to this reality was when rare mating urges overcame him and he was forced to approach his kind. But now things were different. As he wandered he considered what might have been if !Kerrt had not been killed by the two-legged devils. He didn't understand what had changed him. What would he do now that she was gone?

He had wanted to stay near her, but his brief mind contact with the devil known as Hinton had convinced him that these dangerous creatures would be back. He wanted to kill them all! But he realized that when they returned there would be many of them, and they were powerful. He realized that he must leave the area or be killed like !Kerrt.

He slept fitfully and had tormented dreams full of the devils and their ways. He uncharacteristically ignored his bodily needs. "How can I be interested in food with a hole in my heart?" he wondered to himself over and over.

Suddenly a blinding light was all around him. Or was it within his mind? His next sensation was of falling as if the ground under him had disappeared. He fought the spinning sensation of vertigo and its waves of nausea. As he fell he perceived that he was falling toward something that he could just make out in the distance. And then whatever it was, it was upon him, and just as quickly he fell through the thing. He found himself in something like a cave, but it had shimmering walls of nothingness. The cave seemed endless as he moved through it, forever falling toward nothingness.

CHAPTER 27

A door opens in the center of our being and we seem to fall
through it into
immense depths, which, although they are infinite, are all
accessible to us; all
eternity seems to have become ours in this one placid and
breathless contact.
THOMAS MERTON

Alpha Continent

The bright flash of light encompassed Havel and he felt himself spinning and falling. He imagined himself being carried along in the turbulent water of a huge bath tub, circling and heading ever closer to the drain. He saw the *downspout* ahead and almost immediately he was upon it and then through it. He found himself in a shimmering tunnel, whose walls were made of dancing and twisting colors. He couldn't see through the opaque walls. There was a sense of forward movement through the tunnel, but he couldn't be sure the tunnel itself was not moving backward past him, as there was no outer frame of reference. He seemed unable to look "backwards" along the direction from which he had come. As he moved through this strange tunnel he was aware of a distant hum or a ringing sound. Suddenly it occurred to him, "I'm dead! And I'm going through some equivalent of the Psalmist's 'valley of the shadow of death.'" Then his rational mind took over suppressing his panic. "I don't think I'd be so analytic if I were dead and going to heaven," he thought. "Maybe I'm in some type of a wormhole or a

169

travel conduit—but what's the source and where am I going?" In the distance he saw a break in the endless pattern of shimmering energy. He watched the thing grow as it seemed to draw closer to him. It suddenly dawned on him that what he was seeing must be the terminus of the conduit or wormhole.

He exited the thing and found himself in a high mountain meadow ringed by snow-capped peaks. "I know this place!" he said to himself. He recognized it as an idyllic spot on Earth from long ago in his past. He had thought about this place many times since that magical day when he and his best friend came upon it while hiking in the Colorado Rockies. The detail was outstanding and it occurred to him that, "This has to be based on my memory. I can't be back on Earth; this place existed decades ago!"

Havel momentarily suspended his logic and luxuriated in the beauty of the place. A crystal clear stream flowed out of nearby melting snow and cascaded over rocks with a gentle gurgle. The stream ran through the greenest of meadows, full of multicolored wildflowers, and into a small pristine alpine lake. The sky was that deep blue you see from high mountain elevations. "And not a cloud in the sky," he thought wistfully. But there was something different, as he compared the scene to the vision he held in his memory. He looked around and then it came to him. "There's no sun here and there are no shadows!" In the sun's place there was bright light that suffused everything; but it didn't hurt his eyes or make him squint. And the most amazing thing was that the light seemed to come from everywhere and nowhere at the same time.

He was not alone in this place of his memory, or wherever he was. He recognized Tenge and the small alien, whose name mysteriously came to him at that instant, as Roosa. They were both not three meters from him; he was sure they hadn't been there an instant ago. And then suddenly a huge panther-like creature appeared beside them all. Havel observed it to be similar to the description of the aliens encountered by the Beta team! He knew he should be afraid, but strangely he felt no apprehension. He felt completely at peace. In fact, he sensed a bizarre communion with these creatures. He recognized that his feelings were inexplicable as was everything else about this place. He felt such empathy for these other beings who must be at least as confused as he was. As Havel tried to analyze the strange situation, he sensed the mind of another life-form, even though he could not see the being.

Havel felt the touch of Tenge's mind: *Where are we, Captain Havel? Where have you taken us?*

I don't know where we are, Tenge. I don't even know whether this is a real place or one that exists in our minds. And I'm not responsible for this situation; this is far beyond human capacity to engineer. Gesturing with his arm, Havel continued: *This is a place that existed thirty years ago on my home world and is more than fifty light-years from here. The only explanation is that this place isn't real.*

You are partially correct in your assumptions, Captain, came the thoughts of the smaller alien, Roosa. Havel felt the power of her mind. It was beyond anything he had experienced with Tenge. Roosa was more than she seemed to be. "This is no kid," Havel murmured to himself.

Roosa continued: *Each of you is seeing a place that is special to you. Each of you will be able to know the thoughts and feelings of the others in this place.*

I am !Zsakk, came the telepathic roar from the menacing panther that towered above them all. *I don't understand these illusions and I don't trust your lies.* The huge panther shifted toward Havel and bellowed with its mind: *Where are we, Devil? And who are these other creatures? Tell me now or I will crush you one at a time and absorb your thoughts and get the truth!*

Havel was amazed that he didn't feel at all threatened by the great cat that stood at least two meters at its shoulders. He nonchalantly replied: *Well, my name is Captain Havel of the starship Odyssey. This is Tenge and I think that this smaller person is actually in charge of us all. Perhaps you should ask her what all this is about.*

No one controls me, Devil, especially these effete creatures!

Havel met the panther's bared fangs that were above his head and just a half meter from his face. Havel said, *Well, these beings,* gesturing toward Tenge and Roosa, *call themselves the People and they live on the other side of your world, so it doesn't surprise me that you don't know anything about them. And we humans are not Devils as you call us. We are travelers from another world. Some of my companions recently*

171

encountered your species, and perhaps it was you who attacked them, since you seem to know about us.

Liars! You killed my mate and now you try to trick me, bellowed !Zsakk with such a blast of vitriol that Havel couldn't help but wince slightly. Havel could actually feel the panther's hot breath on his face.

Havel had a brief image of himself as if he were in a play exchanging barbs with a thespian's nonchalance that would certainly be uncharacteristic for him. Havel responded: *Actually it was you who attacked my men...!Zsakk. They were only defending themselves. Anyway, I don't think your threats mean much in this place, wherever we are.*

The Captain is correct, came the thoughts of the hidden entity that Havel had sensed. *In this place !Zsakk poses no danger to anyone. This is holy ground and I will not allow any hostile action.* Silently, a shimmering cloud of rainbow colors, dancing with electrical patterns, materialized next to them. As Havel looked at the electric discharges throughout the cloud, he recalled childhood science demonstrations of electricity dancing off a Van de Graaff generator. The roiling and amorphous cloud hovered at shoulder level to Havel. It was hard to guess the cloud's exact dimensions, but Havel guessed it to be perhaps a cubic meter in volume.

The cloud transmitted: *I am Quixt. Do not be shocked by my appearance. My species were once corporeal like you, but eons ago the Progenitor promoted our evolution to this form. I have been working with the People and the Others on this planet for some time. Just as I worked with you Terrans long ago, Captain.*

What do you mean working with Others? came the contemptuous flash from the panther's mind. *No one helps me.*

What arrogance you have, !Zsakk. How little you understand the nature of things, observed the cloud that called itself Quixt.

Havel envisioned the cloud shaking its head in disappointment. Havel thought: *Are you one being or many, Quixt?*

That's an insightful question, Captain Havel. I am one being, but there are many of my kind, many Quixt, working throughout the galaxy.

Havel was again astounded. The implications of this matter of fact statement from Quixt were profound, if true. Here was confirmation that there was life all over the galaxy! "And we humans thought we were special," Havel sighed to himself. *You said you helped humans, Quixt. How?*

We Quixt help promising species make the final leap to sentience. We assist their evolutionary advancement by gently manipulating the neural dendritic connections in the brains of promising life forms. You may be shocked by our actions, but we Quixt consider our work to be sacred.

Havel was becoming a bit uneasy, but he persisted. *So you're saying you helped humans develop by manipulating our brains? Are you God, Quixt?*

Oh no, Captain. I am merely a servant of the Progenitor, or as you say, God. I did help your ancestors a long time ago. The wariness I sense in you is not unusual when a client species learn of its heritage. Some have mistaken our efforts as manipulative or even intrusive, but I assure you that we are directed and driven by a noble cause. I've been in this star system for hundreds of cycles helping Tenge and even you !Zsakk, though none of you has been aware of my subtle touch. In a sense, the Quixt are farmers like you, Tenge. But we farm the stars on behalf of the Progenitor!

Havel found that he was less shocked by the Quixt creature's appearance than his claim of meddling in the development of all of them. But did Quixt's explanation actually answer some fundamental questions? Was there a design behind the universe after all? Havel had always felt that there had to be some reason for the wonders of the universe and especially thoughtful beings. He had often quoted the calculations of a man named Boltzman in the twentieth century. This mathematician purported to compute the improbability of a universe that occurred just by chance, and now exists in all its wonder and complexity fourteen billion years later. Boltzman held that there was one chance in ten to the 80th power (ten with eighty zeros) that their universe occurred by accident! And now this Quixt comes with a startling explanation – actually a revelation, Havel thought.

As he considered the implications of the Design, Havel felt small and insignificant. His vision of humans crossing interstellar space was really inconsequential to the pulse of the universe and the Design described by Quixt. Perhaps he should just discount Quixt's claim; after all it was fantastic in the extreme. But there was a part of Havel that felt reassured and strangely comforted by the assertion that they were *all* part of the grand scheme. And then it hit him in an epiphanal moment, "This is proof of God! God must be the force that is behind everything!" Havel felt a sense of awe and a connection more profound than he had ever imagined. He had always thought that there must be some reason for things, but now he could see the Design if not something of the Designer.

He had so many questions! Havel asked: *You say the Progenitor is known to us as God? Is the Progenitor the first life to become sentient and now exists as an extremely powerful and evolved life? Or is the Progenitor really... God?*

You can trust your feelings, Captain, came the reassuring touch of Quixt's mind. *There are many names for the Progenitor, whom you know as God and the People know as the Maker. !Zsakk does not know the Progenitor. Perhaps that is one reason why we have all been brought here, but I really don't know. I do know that this is a sacred place and we would only be here for a reason; apparently we have a part to play in His Design. This all may seem incredible to you, but what I'm telling you is the truth. I couldn't lie to you in this place of Light, even if I wanted to.*

Roosa rejoined the dialogue, again with her commanding presence: *You are all here because you have the special ability to imagine other places and other possibilities. But there is more. You have all been chosen to hear the Word and to become prophets of the Word. I am the One whom the People have awaited. I am the same "One" known to the Terrans as Jesus. And I am known as the Progenitor to the Quixt. You, !Zsakk, do not know me yet, but you will! And so will the Others of your kind!*

So powerful was the mind and the concepts that a stunned silence hung over the tiny group, broken only by the panting of !Zsakk. A continuous flood of perspectives and relationships flowed from Roosa, and even !Zsakk seemed humbled and submissive.

The rational side of Havel was in a dilemma. "Is this all truth or do I just want to believe this fantastic story? Is it possible that I am being manipulated?" he asked himself. And yet, here he stood on an alien planet (or at least somewhere) among these strange beings and he had to admit that it all felt right on a gut level.

Before Havel could even ask the question, another powerful mind spoke to them, but at a different level. *This is my daughter, Roosa, of whom I am very proud. You are all my children and, yes, you have been brought here for a reason. You are to experience a journey of discovery and wonder. You all represent something unique in my Creation. The People, the Others, and the Terrans all have such unique potential! Because you can see beyond the obvious, I will show you even more! Captain Havel, God is not dead, or irrelevant, as one of your misguided philosophers of the 19th century once opined.*

I have brought you all here at this time and place to make myself known to you in a special way. My desire is that all life forms come of age and know me. In fact, the very purpose of my Creation is that my creatures evolve to a mature understanding of things and then choose relationship with me.

Havel reeled from contact with the powerful mind that could best be understood as the Supreme Being. The flow of ideas and perspectives from that mind was overwhelming. But foremost was the concept that God has many names and has always existed everywhere!

Havel managed to ask: *Creator of all things, why did you choose me? Surely there are others more gifted than me to experience these wonders and hear your message.*

Ah, you Terrans. Only your species would ask "why" of me! I didn't choose you as much as you made the choice to be open to me. Perhaps I should have seen to it that Quixt shaped human development in such a way as to make you less questioning, less obstinate. But it is also your gift to question. This questioning makes your relationship with me dynamic and always new. Captain, even Quixt poses questions to me and struggles with his faith at times. If everything was settled and known, what would be the place of trust or faith? And yet you all do yearn for something, don't you? Each of you senses a need that can only be fully realized in a relationship with Me. Each of you must look for the Way of relationship with me, and then choose it. I want you to know that I am always there, but because I have given you free will you must make the choice to look for Me. Freedom has its benefits and its responsibilities. And it is not necessary that you understand everything. You certainly can't expect to know everything or even control most things. I once told a man on Earth that he could not expect to understand Me or my ways. That man's name was Job, Captain. Perhaps you've heard of him. But I am glad that you chose to seek Me, Captain. Now you and your fellow travelers will see the wonders of my Creation and your destinies!

CHAPTER 23

Then he opened their minds so they could understand.
Luke 24:45
Singularity—A place where there is a rupture of space-time.
BRIAN GREENE from
THE ELEGANT UNIVERSE

Havel abruptly felt the ground give way under him and then he was again falling into another spiraling vortex that quickly plunged them all into a huge wormhole. They fell headlong through the shimmering and twisting tunnel and rapidly exited the terminus. There was a collective mental gasp as they found themselves suspended in interstellar space high above the ecliptic of the Milky Way! They were given extraordinary understanding and they saw from the perspective of God their jewel-like galaxy, floating amidst the vast backdrop of the Cosmos. They saw the hundreds of billions of stars of the galaxy stretched out in spiraling curves like dew drops on the gossamer web of a spider. Their eyes were drawn to the dense galactic center, composed of hundreds of millions of stars, circled by the bejeweled spiral arms of their galactic home. They could see at the center of this mass of brilliance a darkened area that they understood to be a massive black hole. The darkness occurred at the event horizon of the black hole, as its gravity captured the very light emitted by the millions of burning stars collapsing in upon themselves.

They floated in space surrounded by the same encompassing Light they had experienced in the meadow. They were protected from the hard vacuum of interstellar space through an extension of that Love and Grace. Within the protective arms of the Progenitor they reentered the wormhole and fell inward toward the galactic center and its massive black hole. They could see the Progenitor's travel conduit stretched out in front of them across hundreds of thousands of light-years. Havel was in awe and he could only guess the reactions of Tenge and !Zsakk. Havel knew that the Progenitor's travel conduit and protective Light were infinitely more sophisticated than any human contrivance.

They quickly approached the massive black hole and in an instant were across its event horizon. The universe that they knew suddenly winked out of existence, disappearing from their view and their immediate reality.

Downward they fell through time and space that no longer conformed to the realities of their known universe. They were made to *understand* that they were traveling backwards in time toward a universe that was ever younger. They witnessed epoch after epoch as they traveled ever closer to the universe at the Genesis Point. They saw a time when the universe was composed of only ten thousand mega-galaxies. They beheld the time of the first galactic nebulae. Soon they witnessed a time when there was only the maelstrom of elemental charged particles that emerged as the violent energies of Creation cooled and became matter shortly after Planck time. Havel, in this place of expanded awareness, could actually see the relationships between energy and matter and time all predicted by Einstein's equations. Havel and his small group witnessed the expanding massive flux of energy that boiled forth from that Genesis Point, and would become their universe fourteen billion years later.

The Progenitor's wormhole swept them through that fantastic creative fire ever closer to the Genesis Point until they beheld it as a "singularity" at the Dawn of Creation. They understood this point to be more than the place where energy bursts forth to ultimately create a universe of galaxies and creatures. The Genesis Point was not just where something came out of nothing. It was also a gateway to other universes and the transcendent reality of the Progenitor.

The wormhole took them into that singularity and they saw stretching out before them an infinite number of paths that led toward other realities, other possibilities. And they were shown a place of infinite darkness and nothingness, which made them shiver as they beheld a place forever apart from the Progenitor. Havel wanted to ask a question about this dark place, but just as the question was forming, the answer came to them. The Progenitor communicated: *Some souls choose their way rather than the Way. It breaks my heart, but I allow free will and with that comes consequences. If I controlled my children's choices they would be little more than robots and incomplete beings.*

Their fantastic journey continued in a place before space and time, far removed from their world. They saw God *choose* one of the paths and they began to follow it like a long straight road that stretched toward a distant horizon. There was nothing alongside the road; it just seemed suspended in space and rapidly diverged from the other pathways. As they traveled along that road of Creation they watched as God carved energy from the foam of a proto-reality and then formed it into the four fundamental forces of their universe. God selected three dimensions from multiple options and then merged these three with the dimension of time. They witnessed the Design and then the creation of their universe, all at the hand of God.

From the energy released at the Genesis Singularity their universe began, as the energy cooled to first form quarks and then protons, neutrons, electrons and neutrinos. God showed them the organization of elemental matter that led to the atoms of stars and worlds and creatures.

Havel felt like he was on an endless rollercoaster that, with each turn and roll, he didn't think he could stand another twist. But the Progenitor thought otherwise and directed them to look inward: *Now look deep into yourselves.*

Havel looked deeply into the core of his being, into his very soul. And there he saw…God's Singularity at the center of his being! He was tethered to God as a baby is connected to its mother by an umbilical cord. The creative will of God was inculcated into each of them and everything created. Havel saw the essence of the Creator in them as a Spiritual Singularity that existed within all creatures and connected them to the transcendent realm of God.

I exist at the center of the souls of all created beings, the Progenitor uttered. *I created you to need me and to seek me. I give you free will to choose relationship with me and walk in the Light. Or you may refuse Me and exist in darkness. You have been shown my Creation and are given this unique understanding that is only possible at this moment through Me. You will soon return to your time and your worlds. You will remember something of this journey, but the details will fade because your minds are not capable of grasping these concepts without my help. Over time it is my wish that your species move ever closer to Me. I have made you in such a way that you all have the urge to seek Me. Like moths fluttering toward a light, you have a desire to fly close to my warmth. Sometimes you will feel close to my Light and bask in its warmth. Sometimes you will stray into the darkness, but each time you will feel drawn back to me. I show you these things because I have chosen each of you to be my voice to your people. This will at times be hard, but know that I am with you. You have but to sit quietly and listen for the music of the ages resonating from the Spiritual Singularity in your souls, to know that I am with you always!*

Havel awoke lying on the meeting field with the sensation that only an instant had passed, despite their journey through time and space. He was lying next to Tenge who was also awakening. Roosa was still standing beside them as if she hadn't moved. As he looked around there was no sign of !Zsakk. And Havel could no longer see the Quixt entity. They were surrounded by an opalescent bubble through which he could just make out Dr. Walker who seemed to be shouting at him. Havel couldn't hear what Walker was saying.

Havel felt Quixt's mind reach out to the Progenitor: *Oh, Lord, thank you for these visions and all that I am. I pray that I will always serve you.*

Yes, my Quixt, you will continue in my service. You will again travel the stars doing my bidding, but now you will go with the assurance that you are never alone. My spirit is within you and in all creatures.

The Progenitor continued: *But Quixt, you still have some confusion about Roosa. You still do not see the relationship. Listen to me well, my faithful servant. I was Jesus long ago on Earth. And I am here now as Roosa. She and I are one. And I will continue to manifest myself over and over to other beings as they reach maturity.*

Havel smiled as he sensed Quixt's struggle to see Roosa as the latest incarnation of God, the Progenitor. Havel couldn't fault Quixt. Havel himself had always thought of God as spirit. It was a bit unsettling to consider God as a physical being. He wondered if the ancients had felt similarly in Jesus' presence. He thought to himself, "I wonder what it is like for God to live as a creature, even if only for a short time? It must be so limiting and such a sacrifice to give up so much for the benefit of the created. It could only be done out of supreme love." Havel recalled the Greek word *agape* that signified a sacrificial type of love. He thought, "Surely incarnation is the ultimate expression of agape. And to witness the latest incarnation is an...epiphany!"

Roosa turned to Tenge. *Father of mine, we have much work to do for our People. Don't you agree?*

Bowing his head and then lifting his eyes with pride and reverence, Tenge considered his daughter. She, who had always been his purpose for living, now had become his destiny as well. *Yes, we do, Roosa. We have much to do and much to tell.*

And Captain, continued the Progenitor who spoke from within Roosa, *I expect you and the Terrans to help me with the People and with the Others.*

Havel bowed his head as the energy bubble faded. He said: *Who in his right mind could say no to You?*

Each person is born with an unencumbered spot...an umbilical
spot of
Grace where we were first touched by God.
MARK NEPO

EPILOGUE

God is the spiritual centered point.
ARISTOTLE

Beta Continent

!Zsakk awakened alert and very rested. It was as if he had slept a full cycle and had a full belly. In fact, he felt wonderful, even invigorated. And his energy stores were completely restored for the first time in many cycles. He couldn't understand why that should be so because he hadn't eaten in some time.

And then he began to recall his *dream*. "What a weird dream," he thought. "It's like something happened to me." As he considered the strange visions, he also wondered why this dream seemed to linger and seemed so real. "Most dreams fade so quickly," he mused.

Unexpectedly he sensed the thoughts of an Ela herd not two hundred meters from his lair, and they were coming his way. Well-honed reflexes were kindled as he prepared himself for the hunt. And yet, he hesitated. In the thoughts of the Ela he sensed a pattern that he struggled to recognize.

As he considered the Ela, he was abruptly distracted by a flash low in the western sky, followed momentarily by a muffled thunderclap. He looked in the direction of the flash and saw, coming straight toward him, a flying object. But this was no bird or animal that he had ever seen.

A powerful mind then touched his and he remembered!

!Zsakk, I'm coming to you and the Others. I'm with the Terrans and we bring you glad tidings of great joy!

He recognized the thought patterns. These were the thoughts of Roosa, the being who was in his dream! And in a flash the complete events and the journey replayed in his mind. This was not a dream and the Roosa creature was coming to see him! He managed to wonder, "What's happening to me?"

He staggered as his mind flooded with the profound complexities of his new understanding of reality. Just a short time ago he had abandoned his solipsistic philosophy to embrace a relationship with !Kerrt. Then he encountered the human creatures that killed his love one. Yet he discovered that he could not hate them because he now understood so much more. They weren't really Devils after all. But even this was eclipsed by the revelation of a Supreme Being, personified as Roosa, who was now coming to see him!

"This is just too much," he thought as he shook his head. "I just can't deal with all this."

And then it further dawned on him that the elusive thought pattern emanating from the Ela herd was again that of Roosa! He saw the herd that had now moved to the clearing's edge. They showed no fear of him. In fact they were watching him with bright, almost laughing, eyes. The improbable dream was not only real, but the spirit of the Supreme Being was embodied in the Ela and was reaching out to him!

"Are you sure this is wise, Captain?" whispered the recovered Steve Hinton from the navigator's chair of the landing craft. "These beasts are intelligent and very dangerous. We still know so little about them. And how do you expect to find one panther in the middle of this huge continent?"

Havel turned slowly in the co-pilot's chair to look into the deep yellow eyes of Roosa sitting in the second row of the landing craft. Their minds touched and Havel returned his gaze to the forward window as he scanned the instruments and the jungle below.

"We won't have any trouble finding him, Commander because Roosa has already contacted !Zsakk. He knows we're coming and we're in no danger. For the first time in his life !Zsakk has a purpose and realizes he's connected to everything, even to us. Havel grinned at his perplexed executive officer. Relax, Steve, something wonderful is about to happen... again!"

> Hope is a thing with feathers that perches in the soul.
> EMILY DICKINSON

Printed in the United States
201385BV00003B/349-390/P